About *Searching the Heart of God*

"John Capellaro and Patti Davis spiritual resource. Written for a varie_ _____, _____ _____ _____ who preach, those who value the spiritual life, and those who enjoy entertaining the well formed sermon, the book's compelling narrative invites engagement. For the harried and unhappily empty preacher – and who among us has not been in this place? – the book might offer a respite for new ideas. For those poor in spirit or hopeful in spirit, this collection might provide a place of solace, comfort and renewal. Any one homily can be thoughtfully read in ten minutes. In such devotional times I can see moments of worship coming quite near.

"So what resources constitute this book? A collection of sermons organized according to five of the major seasons of the church year, the individual sermons paint bright pictures of seasonal preaching possibilities. 'Words are powerful,' the authors write, 'and the carefully chosen or the thoughtlessly spoken can work changes in us that persist long after their sound has died.' As this quote suggests, the authors write with an expressive and expectant style.

"The Table of Contents itself offers the reader a kind of roadmap to the Christian year and to the book's contents. For example, in Epiphany sermons range from 'Fig Tree Time' to 'God in a Box,' both of which catch a possible facet in the diamond of this Season of Light. Among others St. Anselm makes a helpful appearance, and current news stories offer places to ground Gospel in the midst of the life contemporary Christians daily live.

"The sermons presented are not preachy, they lift the spirit, providing the reader with unexpected perspectives in the midst of the old, old story of God's love for us. Strongly sacramental, these homilies seek to explore in the outward and visible signs of life those inward and spiritual graces as near to us, always, as breath to lungs. Every reader will likely appreciate this gift from the authors."

Howard Hanchey

An Episcopal priest and retired Arthur Lee Kinsolving Professor of Pastoral Theology at the Virginia Theological Seminary in Alexandria, Virginia, Howard Hanchey is the author of several widely used books pertaining to Sunday morning Christian education, evangelism, and studies in church growth and effective church leadership.

EARCHING
HE HEART OF GOD

DEACON AND PRIEST IN CONVERSATION

SEARCHING
THE HEART OF GOD

DEACON AND PRIEST IN CONVERSATION

patricia rhoads davis
john j. capellaro

ISBN: 1-932009-74-4

FIRST EDITION

Published July 2003

Greene Tree Publications
C/O Crippen & Landru Publishers
P. O. Box 9315
Norfolk, VA 23505
USA

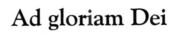

Ad gloriam Dei

Acknowledgments

None of us goes through this life alone. When we recognize the truth that all accomplishments are the result of the gracious offering of many gifts from many gifted people, we cannot help but respond in thanksgiving. Especially, we are indebted to Doug Greene whose vision of this book has been persistent and persuasive and has brought it to fruition while working with preachers prone to distraction and delay. Genevieve Zetlan, Principal of Nimble Communications, LLC, is equally capable of vision, translating our ill-formed dreams of God into a visual expression in dramatic cover art. The congregation of St. Paul's Episcopal Church in Norfolk, Virginia has been the impetus and inspiration for our struggle to use words in a way that transcends the few minutes on a Sunday morning in which they are actually heard. Their requests for copies, their constructive feedback and even their arguments with the message push us to probe the heart of God further, a never-ending spiritual journey which we joyfully take together.

Finally, we must thank our spouses, Bernadette Capellaro and Rod Davis, whose endless rereading, helpful suggestions and infinite patience with us testify to their singular devotion to partnership in the amazing journey that is ordained ministry.

John J. Capellaro
Patricia Rhoads Davis

Contents

Pentecost

Extra Ordinary Times

Foreword

To publish a book of sermons is to act with some presumption. It is to presume that at this time and place in space and history, we have something worth preserving and passing on. It is to recognize that in words, there is a power worth sharing, a message in need of another medium. So it is that we approach this book with trepidation and awe, with prayers for God's spirit to continue to move on the written page as He moves so powerfully on a Sunday morning, to move our hearts to love and our bodies to action.

Because words are powerful. The carefully chosen, or the thoughtlessly spoken, word can work changes in the heart that persist long after the sound has died. And for as long as people have been talking, we have been using words to tell the stories that define our lives and in doing so, transmit something of who we are in relation to creation and the Creator. And who we are in relationship to each other. These sermons are offered particularly as a reflection of our shared ministry, priest and deacon considering together God's action in the world and our response. It is a ministry we have joyfully shared for some three and a half years now, a ministry that has been wonderfully surprising. We have learned anew what our Lord had in mind at creation when he deigned that it was not good to be alone. In shared ministry we are both the better for it and hope that is evident in sermons that reveal our deepening understanding of the ministry to which we are all called, as servants of Christ.

ADVENT AND CHRISTMAS

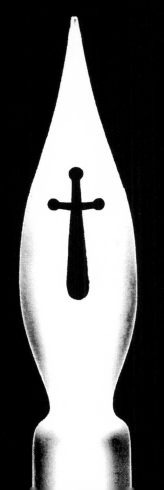

Please Make It Real!

Season of Advent – John J. Capellaro

When John heard in prison what the Messiah was doing, he sent word by his disciples and said to him, "Are you the one who is to come, or are we to wait for another?" Matthew 11:2-3

The long-awaited rain quickly soaks the hard, dry ground and begins to seep through the walls of John's prison cell. He had preached about water many times; he'd spent long hours standing in it, baptizing hundreds who had accepted his message of repentance and new life. But now somehow – the passion and purpose that had driven him to that life – are absent. The water continues to trickle into his cell and a small pool of mud begins to form. He puts his fingers into the mud and makes swirls and patterns in it; he gets a wad of it on the ends of his fingers and smears it on the back of his hand. As he plays, he feels the muscles of his face form into a smile – and as he does, he begins to remember the events that have led him to this prison cell.

He remembers his father, Zechariah – a priest: a man who said God had called him. It's where John first learned about being called by God. He remembers how his father had been struck mute during his mother's pregnancy with him, because he didn't believe the vision that predicted his son's birth – at first – the same vision that instructed Zechariah to name his son, John. His father told John that story many times growing up – especially around the time of John's birthday. John's favorite part of the story was how when it came time for his father to name him, everyone expected him to name him Zechariah, but his mute father motioned for a writing-tablet and wrote, "His name is John." At that moment his father was able to speak. The first words his father said were, "Blessed be the Lord God of Israel …" and then he said a very long prayer of praise – a prayer which John learned as a boy and in his cell now repeats out loud as he squats in the dirt. He is grateful for the prayer his father taught him. He is still awed by his family stories – by his father and how seriously he took his "calls" from God. "It's odd how so many dismiss those things in their lives that seem to be from God, and forget to make them part of their family story," John thinks to himself.

John remembers his mother, Elizabeth, and his smile broadens. He remembers the story that his mother told him over and over as a boy – about that time during her pregnancy with him that Mary came for a visit – who was also pregnant at the time with her firstborn son, Jesus. And how when Mary greeted Elizabeth, she said, "John leaped for joy in her womb – to be in the presence of their Lord." That's what she said. "Even before I was born, I knew Jesus? Did I?" For a moment John is refreshed in his sense of call. He then remembers the encounter with Jesus at the River Jordan, where he baptized this man that should have baptized him – and how at the moment of Jesus' baptism several of them had heard a voice from heaven saying, "This is my son, the Beloved. With him I am well pleased." His memory is clear; he knows Jesus; he is clear about who he is, and has been since before his own birth. "I've lived as faithfully as I know how," he said out loud, as if he were still alone in the desert. "I'm in this cell, because I've been faithful to my call – a call to prepare the way for God to do a new thing. I'm in this cell because I have trusted that God is moving me to something within reach and yet beyond comprehension."

Just then his knees and back stiffen, and John stands up to take a breath in his cell. The stench of his cell is momentarily cleansed by the smell of new rain. And now John's newfound confidence is shaken without warning, as if all his stories – all his remembrances are madness. He leans over once more and grabs a handful of mud and rubs it between his hands. "This is real! No visions or voice from heaven; no leaping babies in mother's womb. The mud is real – just as real as whatever Herod is going to do with me." He savors the mud, smells it, and wonders about so much – with a loud groan.

His moment of private torment is interrupted by the arrival of four friends. The guard opens John's cell, and they enter – all with empty looks on their faces. John wipes his hands on the wet wall and tells them how glad he is to see them. They want to know what John knows of his future, and he tells them he knows nothing of Herod's intentions. They ask John what they might do for him, and he answers, "Only one thing."

He then looks at the mud on his hands, smells the clean rain, considers all he knows from his father, his mother, and his own life – looks at his friends, and says to them, "Go to Jesus – and ask him if he's really the one. Ask him if he's the one for whom we have waited. Ask him if he is The One." The pressing weight of fear and uncertainty halts his breathing, and his throat tightens. His smile fades and his most prominent feature becomes his weakness. His disciples embrace him and leave without a word.

We don't know if John ever got to hear Jesus' answer because for Matthew – it is beside the point. It's not about discovering proof of Jesus as Messiah. It's not about certainty. It never was. Faith has little to do with belief. We've had those ideas confused for centuries. It's about John's decision – it's about our decision. It's about choosing to trust in the absence of proof. That's faith. It's about embracing the inevitable doubts that arise – when we take the time to think, pray and wonder – sometimes with deep groans. It's about staying with the call that God offers every one of us – that call that moves us towards something – within reach and yet beyond comprehension. We, like John, have a choice to make. We are all called. We can ignore God's call – pretend it's too vague for us – explain away the signs – focus only on the mud. Or we can live in trust – not fearing our doubts, but knowing that without doubt there is no such thing as faith.

The Feast of Christmas is upon us. Can we look more deeply into the charming story our children reenact for us and find our part in the story? Can we find the beginning of our new history? Our faith is good enough. It is no worse than John the Baptist's. Are we willing to hear God's call and trust in God – again?

The Rainbow and the Mud

Season of Advent – Patricia R. Davis

For as the days of Noah were, so will be the coming of the Son of Man ... Therefore you must be ready, for the Son of Man is coming at an unexpected hour.   Matthew 24:37-44

One of the problems with using the lectionary is that we seldom get to look at the Old Testament stories in any depth. The very stories that are the foundation of our faith, that color our own faith stories, are assumed to be familiar, without any refreshing our memory as to why they're important. But in today's Gospel lesson Jesus makes reference to the days of Noah, which is the perfect piece of permission for looking at a story that gets lost in the mists of myth, one we've all heard of but seldom examined.

Maybe you remember it from Sunday school as a child, how everyone in the world was so evil that God regretted his creation and decided to start over again. We can identify with that part – maybe. It's as though we go to paint the living room and the color on the little swatch was so pretty but when we get it on the wall it's this awful shade of teal or hot pink or something that's an obvious mistake, so rather than live with it we cover the whole thing over with a flood of fresh paint.

But God found one part of his creation that he liked fairly well, and that was Noah. The Bible says he *was a righteous man, blameless in his generation.* Well, that's about as good as it gets this side of heaven, so God instructed Noah to build a large boat and put all his family in it along with a matched set of every animal on the earth. Then God sent a terrific flood that wiped out everyone and everything that wasn't on the ark ... rain and rain and more rain, and if you think of endless summer

18

days of heat and sticky, oppressive humidity, you'll have an idea of what that experience was like! So there were days and days of rain and then months of riding this claustrophobic, stinky boat before the water finally receded enough for Noah and his passengers to light on solid, if muddy, ground and begin again to make a life for themselves. Well, God must have been doing some thinking during all this time Noah was riding the waves because when it was all over, God made a rainbow as a sign of a new covenant between them ... that covenant being that Noah would be the new Adam, starting creation all over again and God wouldn't ever go to such drastic extremes to set things right again.

OK, that's the story. Now let's look at who Noah really was. What strikes me about him is his utter lack of imagination. He's not a hero or a visionary. He doesn't question God, except maybe to ask *How long is a cubit*, he doesn't stick up for his neighbors, say *Wait a minute, some of these people who will be drowned are my friends, my neighbors.* He doesn't argue, like Abraham, that the existence of one righteous man should be enough to preserve the world; he doesn't offer, like Jesus, to take the place of all those who will die. He just goes about building this big boat and to heck with the rest of the world. It doesn't sound very righteous to me, but, then, I'm not God. He is, however, willing to trust in God's strange request, trust not only his own life but that of his whole family. He doesn't reject the idea of doing a strange and apparently foolish thing simply because it's too crazy to really believe that God would ask it.

So here we have what is really a pretty ordinary man, in other words, a mixed bag of good and bad. He's ordinary in the same way as the two women grinding meal or the homeowner who finally goes off to bed in our gospel story. Ordinary in the same way that most of us are most of the time, doing our best to get through the days doing what we need to do, whether it's building a boat or grinding meal or getting the kids off to school. And then God comes into Noah's life in a way that can't be ignored and everything changes. You'd think that after such an experience, witnessing the end of the world as he knew it, that Noah would indeed be a thoroughly changed man.

But as soon as he steps off the ark, he steps into mud and muck. And instead of trusting the rainbow, which was God's promise, and God's obvious care for him in his salvation so far, Noah immediately offers a sacrifice to an angry God and then goes off and gets drunk. And when one of his sons sees him in a less than dignified state, Noah curses him and his children, and the whole human mess that is this world picks up right where we left off *before* the flood.

And that's the crux of the problem as I see it. We go through some life-changing experience, maybe something as dramatic as a life-threatening illness or military combat or an automobile accident or Sept. 11th, and we think, *from now on, things will be different. I'm not going to waste my time on unimportant things any more. I'm going to focus on what really matters and be thankful every day of my life.* And we're good at it for a little while but before you know it, there we are, cursing at the traffic and yelling at the kids and thinking our boss is several bricks shy of a full load. We're asleep while the thief breaks in and steals our souls. We've forgotten the people outside the ark.

So when we hear the story of Noah, I think we need to hear a story not just about being ready, but a story about our tendency to go through life besotted by our own concerns, unable to remember the rainbow in the sky. Because if we remember that rainbow, then we're forced to remember that the life we live, we live by the grace of God. We're forced to remember that it's the sign of a covenant initiated by God that means more than the promise of preservation, it means the promise of God's care and nurture, no matter what we do. God absolutely will not abandon the world ever again.

So, if we are a covenant people, if we are people who believe, then our obligation is to respond as that kind of people. The way we can avoid being drowned by our own concerns is by remembering that we're not on the ark anymore with a selected group of agreeable companions. We're on muddy ground with a motley crew of people who are all trying not to trip after going through some life-changing experiences. For this time in the story, **we** are the new Adam, just off the ark. And while there's certainly plenty of personal clean-up work to do, we simply cannot keep our heads down, grinding away. We cannot fall asleep. If we're at all bound by a covenant of belief, it's up to us to help the man who stumbles and the woman who trips over rocky ground and the child who's lost.

We can't know the time when Jesus will come again. The only thing we can do is be ready. And to my mind, being ready means acting like the people we are, people of an old *and* a new covenant. So that when we get up in the morning, we look for the rainbow and not the mud. So that when we look in another person's eyes, we see the rainbow and not the mud. So that when we decide how to spend our days, we are looking for the rainbow and not the mud. We must so act like changed people that others notice. That people pause from slogging through the mud to look up and see what we have seen, the rainbow ... and the cross. *Amen.*

You're Nothing But a Loser!

Season of Advent – John J. Capellaro

And the angel Gabriel came to her and said, "Greetings, favored one! The Lord is with you."   Luke 1:28

Do you know something? We're all a bunch of *losers* – when we're at our best, that is! A few years ago an Episcopal Church in Manhattan ran a series of ads in the subway stations surrounding the neighborhood that gained national recognition. One of those ads had a very simple headline – in huge letters: BECOME A LOSER.

The rest of the copy was in small print, so that you had to walk from the edge of the subway platform over to the ad, bend down and read. It went something like:

Become a Loser.

If you're looking for how to give up the things in this world that keep you from being the best you can be, come visit us.

We'll help you lose your old life and discover a new one.

After all, Jesus Christ lost everything. And he gained the whole world.

Get a life.

Discover the Episcopal Church of the Heavenly Rest

Losers. It's what we all are – when we are at our best. We are a people called to lose the things that weigh us down: our professional competence, our credentials, our pedigrees, and get free – so we can live. God loves losers. God has kinship with losers. God can work through losers. God would never be a Virginia Tech fan.[1] It's that familiar motif of finding strength in our weakness; discovering sight in our blindness; finding new life out of death. Funny how God is so disposed towards those the world calls losers.

A long time ago, there lived a young unmarried woman named Mary. Mary became pregnant and was scorned by most who knew her, and so she moved. She moved into the vacant house at the end of our street in Willow Grove, Pennsylvania. It was 1959, and we were living in one of those post war housing developments, where the houses were affordable and all looked alike. Our community was comprised of two streets that paralleled each other – each street with fourteen identical houses. They were made different from one another only by the addition of a back porch or in landscaping details. We took pride in our neighborhood. Most people knew each other; I think every child in the neighborhood attended St. John of the Cross parochial school – and nearly everyone went to church there too – except, that is, for Mary – that new woman who moved into the house at the end of our street. She didn't go to church at all. In fact, she never seemed to leave the house. But everyone had heard that she was pregnant and unmarried.

An older man with a beard used to come and spend a few days at a time there with Mary, and the neighborhood speculated that he was her lover. It all made for great mystery and adventure for us children. At age ten I was keenly aware of the "problem" this woman was for the neighborhood. She didn't fit in. After school, as we gathered at a friend's house, we could hear parents talking about "that woman," and how she was letting her house go to seed – and how it was going to effect the value of our homes, and how she was pregnant and had no husband – and how she had this mysterious male visitor – with a beard! My friends and I learned quickly that it was okay to make fun of this woman. And so we did, as did most everyone in the neighborhood. Mary's house

---

[1] At the time of this sermon, Virginia Tech's football team was moving towards a national championship.

was the only one in our neighborhood that got hit by our older brothers on *Mischief Night* – the night before Halloween when you soap up windows, knock down mailboxes, ring doorbells and run away. There was an unspoken conspiracy between parents and children that Mary's house and reputation was fair game for all. She was a loser.

One day after school, two of my ten-year-old friends and I were sitting on Mary's lawn playing with matches. We'd never sit on anyone else's lawn without permission – but we didn't need permission to sit on Mary's lawn – she was a loser. Her lawn had become overgrown with grass tall enough to come up to our shoulders. We were playing with matches and accidentally set Mary's lawn on fire. Thankfully, we were able to extinguish the fire by sliding up and down the terraced lawn and extinguishing the fire with our backsides – but not before half Mary's lawn was charred. As we ran away – laughing wildly – we could see Mary looking out her window at us. When my friend's parents heard about our escapades they decided that they'd had enough of this Mary. If she took care of her lawn this wouldn't have happened. My friend didn't even get scolded for playing with matches and they agreed not to tell my parents. We knew something was very special about this Mary.

A neighborhood meeting was called and since no one could afford such luxuries as babysitters, all the children attended as well. I remember parents saying things like, "We've worked hard to keep our property up. How do you think we feel when we see that dump? And besides, she's pregnant and not even married. How will living near *that* effect our children?" It's remarkable how easily momentum can build in situations like this. As one of the more fervent speeches about God, home and country was being delivered, a sudden quiet came over the gathering. We turned to see Mary standing in the doorway. She came inside and told everyone that she knew she hadn't kept her place up, and that she was sorry about that. The man we'd seen coming and going was her brother, who had helped her buy the house, and he was due to arrive again later that week to help her with the lawn, clean up a little and then help Mary move in with him and his family in New Jersey. Her pregnancy wasn't going well, and that's why she hadn't done much work around the house; she was supposed to be in bed. The house was going up for sale, she told us, and she was very sorry for the troubles that she brought to us during her time in the neighborhood. She couldn't have been more than twenty, and I remember how beautiful she looked with her big belly. I remember how gently she spoke and I remember feeling shame – perhaps more clearly than ever before in my life. And if the silence that endured after her departure was any indication, I think even the adults felt shame. I think our whole neighborhood learned something that night. God had done something important through this young woman – this Mary – this loser. God loves Losers. God has kinship with losers. God can work through losers.

The Mary we hear about in our Bible story today is another loser – another young, unmarried, pregnant woman – who endures the taunts of her neighbors, and the whispers of intolerance from the church community. Even her son, Jesus, the one we call Lord, is just another loser: a boy comes into the world through a lineage of losers: unfaithful men, unmarried women, and outcasts; a boy who will grow up to have a flash in the pan ministry – with big talk – that gets him nothing but execution at the hands of the Roman authorities: a loser in whom God is perfectly revealed; a loser who leaves as a legacy a few women and men who carry on his message in the face of futility. But we shouldn't be surprised. They're nothing but a bunch of losers. God loves losers. God has kinship with losers. God can work through losers.

This world is full of losers – always has been. But some are easier to spot than others. I was at Maury High School the other night for a meeting designed to help parents learn how to fill out Federal Financial Aid forms that colleges require to award scholarships. The forms seemed easy enough I thought, until the questions started coming from the audience. One young girl, who was obviously a student, asked, "I'm 18 years old; I live with my cousins. I don't have a father, and my mother is incarcerated. What do I put on the lines that ask for parents' names and income?" As I turned to see who was asking the question, I could see several students who were there alone – without parents, working with each other to figure out these forms. Losers. That's what they are: easy to spot losers. And my hunch is that God has a keen interest in them – and may be doing remarkable work through them – if we'd only listen and learn.

Then there are the not so easy to spot losers: like folks who come to church on Sundays, dressed up real nice, presenting facades of tremendous professional competence, impressive credentials, and illustrious pedigrees – who inside may be hurting deeply due to the loss of a loved one – or feel like there isn't one more ounce of energy left for life – because of a marriage that's a mess; or be carrying around enormous bags of anger – because something that's wanted more than anything in the world is beyond reach. Losers, that's all they are: losers. Well, you're in good company. God loves losers. *"Greetings favored one. The Lord is with you!"* God may be ready to do something miraculous through you. God may even be ready to do something miraculous – *in* you. Become a Loser this Christmas. Join the ranks of millions who have discovered the promise to be found in losing your life and following the Prince of all losers. Get a real life. Become a Loser! *Amen.*

A Shepherd's Tale

Christmas Eve – Patricia R. Davis

In that region there were shepherds living in the fields, keeping watch over their flock by night.   Luke 2:1-20

"I'm an old man now," said the shepherd, "and I don't have too many days left to me. Perhaps you're not interested in hearing the story of a forgetful old man, but I have to tell it. My wife and children are sick of hearing me talk about it, and my brothers are all dead now but if you've got time to listen, I'd like to tell you a story. I'll be gone one of these days, you know, so I want to tell you what happened to me one night a long time ago. Do you have time to listen? I know I've told it before but listen one more time, just in case I've left something out. Listen…

"I was a young man then, not bent and crippled like I am now. I was young and strong and very successful as shepherds go, with a large flock of the best sheep, healthy and beautiful they were, with the finest wool and the softest faces. I often sold them to pilgrims who wanted to make a sacrifice in the temple, and the lambs for Passover, of course. So I made a good living and my wife and children wanted for nothing, so far as I could give it. But still, I was just a shepherd, so maybe what I have to say won't seem that important. Maybe you won't take the word of a simple shepherd when there are so many people wiser and better educated than I. But I have to tell you my story because maybe then you'll know what it is to be a shepherd who is more than a shepherd, on the inside.

"It was more than 50 years ago now, and, like I said, I was a young man, young and strong. My brothers and I took good care of the sheep, they were our livelihood after all, and so on this night we were in the

27

fields, watching out for them. The sheep were all inside the enclosure for the night, the rocks made a sort of natural pen and we had a gate at one end we could close off. We sat a little ways off, except for my brother, Simon, who liked to lie down next to the sheep in their pen to keep warm. My shepherd's crook was close at hand, should any wolves come looking for an easy meal, but this night it was quiet.

"When I think back on it, I should have noticed that it was too quiet. All those people streaming down the road toward Bethlehem day and night, with their animals and their children, all those people jostling to get into the city for the census. It had been so noisy all day long that I should have noticed the quiet but I only thought what a blessed relief, to have the day's work done, to be able to sit in peace, all the animals watered and fed and me too, with a good meal of bread and cheese in my stomach to get me through the night. Well, like I said, I should have noticed the quiet, but you know how it is. When you've been busy all day long and you finally get to sit and just be. Your mind goes blank and you wrap up in your cloak and just sit there. Time passes and you realize you've been looking but not seeing, just drifting away to another place for a while.

"Like I said, it was quiet and if I hadn't been so sleepy, I might have noticed it was more like that quiet before the storm than the quiet after one, but I was tired. And it was cold. So maybe I wasn't thinking clearly, maybe what I tell you now will seem like nothing more than a dream except it wasn't a dream. I was sitting on the ground, my back against a tree, lest some animal sneak up behind me, leaning against a tree and drifting off, when I heard what sounded like thunder. Now mind you, it was clear that night, not a cloud in the sky so it couldn't have been thunder, could it? But it was something like that, a low rumble that got louder and louder so then I was wide-awake and trying to figure out what was going on. The sheep moved around in the pen and started bleating; they were afraid of something and it scared me too. And then the sound changed. First it was a rumble, like thunder, now it was a soft rustling, like the beating of a thousand doves' wings. And where before the sky had been the same sky I see every night, all the stars in their places, now the sky just exploded, stars flying across the heavens from east to west, just flying I tell you, a cascade of stars. And something came over me; it was like a song running through my head. All I could think was, 'Glory to God in the highest.' Over and over, 'Glory be to God.' And I wasn't afraid any more and the sheep got quiet again and that's all there was to it, except there was more.

"Because something told me I had to go into Bethlehem, something moved me to take off running for the city, a crazy piece of behavior, I tell you, except that my brothers must have felt it too because I looked back and saw them running after me, running as though our lives depended on it. I didn't know why I was running or even where I was running to but I kept running, into town, past inns still open for late arriving pilgrims, past houses shuttered for the night, past shops and stores, running until suddenly I stood at the entrance to a sort of cave, behind a small inn. I still don't know how I got there but there I was and that quiet was there too. That quiet before the storm, you could feel it.

"There was a woman inside the cave, a woman on the straw, among the animals quartered there for the night. She was lying on the straw with her head in her husband's lap and it was the saddest, prettiest picture I ever saw. It was obvious she had just given birth; the baby lay in a stone trough beside her, the nearest thing to a cradle for a woman worn out by life's hardest labor."

"And then I began to feel foolish. Here I was, panting and out of breath, I'd run a mile or more, I must have lost my mind, run a mile or more and ended up in a barn just to see a woman I didn't know and her new baby. I felt foolish and an intruder, too. Childbirth should be a private time, not an opportunity for strangers to come and gawk, as though we had anything to do with it, as though she needed us to witness to the birth of her first-born son. But there she was and there we were and I stood and stared and apologized for disturbing them but something compelled me to come closer. His mother didn't ask me to leave, or his father either, for that matter; perhaps they were too exhausted to care but I went closer. Something about that baby, lying in the straw, drew me closer. Now I've seen plenty of babies; I had nine of my own, so why another baby should be so interesting I don't know.

"Now maybe it was just the shadows thrown by the lantern. Maybe it was just that I had been so tired and sleepy and then suddenly scared that I was imagining things. It was just a baby after all. But there was something about him that took my breath away. First it was his eyes. He looked at me, and even though I know that babies don't really see anything clearly for some weeks anyway, I could have sworn that he could see me clearly, could see into my very soul. His look almost hurt, it was so deep and, I could swear, that baby looked like he loved me. And there was something else. Now I'm not a superstitious man. I leave signs and wonders and fortune telling to those with more money than sense, but I swear to you, by everything that's holy, that on this baby boy I saw something. And it made me gasp and feel afraid again, for just a moment, though maybe it was just the bruising that you sometimes see on infants after birth. But anyway, I saw something on his forehead. Maybe it was just a shadow, like I said, but his forehead looked bruised, and his eyes beneath, like I told you, they looked at me.

Then suddenly I knew I had to get out of there, go back to the fields and the sheep and everything just the way it is supposed to be, go back and try to come to grips with what I had seen and felt. Maybe in the clear light of day it would all make sense. What a crazy night! But it didn't seem right to just leave after standing there and gaping like some insane tourist, so I gave the boy's father my shepherd's staff. Maybe it would come in handy to protect the boy, because it seemed to me that this life is hard enough without starting out with the marks of pain already on your forehead. So I gave his father my staff and then we left, my brothers and I. We walked back to the sheep, not talking, till about halfway back, when I let out a cry of sheer joy. I don't know where it came from. We'd just been to see a new baby after all, nothing remarkable in that, babies are born all the time, but man, it felt so good to have been there!

"That's my story, that's all there is to it, the ramblings of an old man who doesn't think too clearly anymore. I've forgotten so much now but this much I remember: a tired mother, held by her husband, and a baby lying in the straw, with the shadow of death on his forehead and life in his eyes. It was a crazy night, I can tell you that, but I was there and I saw it and, I've never forgotten. Just a baby boy, with the shadow of death on his forehead and life in his eyes."

Successful Lives

Christmas Eve – John J. Capellaro

"… the least among all of you is the greatest." *Luke 9:48*

Katherine came from Charleston and a good family – a family with a history and many successes to their credit. She was attractive and had the benefits of a good education and a supportive family. Upon graduation from Law School, she joined a prestigious law firm, which required her to take a sojourn away from home in Columbia, South Carolina. She set a new high for first year salaries at that firm – male or female. A few years later, while visiting family in Charleston, she met a young man and married him – married well, as the expression goes – an architect, named Simon, who understood historical restoration at a genetic level. His father, grandfather, and great grandfather were all architects. After the wedding, they settled back home in Charleston in one of *his* family properties downtown, just a few blocks from the water that offered a view of Old Fort Sumter. There they began their charmed life. She and her new husband were the talk of the town.

Their first child was born eight years after their marriage, just about when they'd planned to begin their family. It was a boy. They named him Simon. Dad was already talking architect. They had the best doctors, and of course little Simon was brought home from the hospital in a special gown that had been in the family for generations. The boy grew up, attended the best private schools, and distinguished himself in soccer, tennis, and mathematics. He had a flair for the arts, and loved visiting the cathedrals of Europe with his parents; the frescoes and music inspired him. He knew that someday *he* would create something grand – and that he would carry on many, many great traditions.

Mary came from a town that had been the subject of jokes for decades. Nazareth was poor and unsophisticated, as were its residents. There wasn't much of a future here for anyone, especially an unwed, pregnant, teenager. She and Joseph, the poor fool that said he'd marry her – even though it wasn't his baby – were now the subject of jokes from a townspeople that knew something about cruel jokes. She and her new husband were the talk of the town. Their first child was born even before the marriage ceremony, while on a journey to Joseph's hometown. This was not at all how Joseph or Mary had planned things. It was a boy. They named him Jesus *(In Hebrew, Jeshua – "God Saves")*. He was born in a cave that was used as a stable; they wrapped him in bands of cloth, as was the custom, to keep the body straight and ensure proper growth. The baby was then laid in a simple feeding trough in the cave. Some local shepherds visited them, and told them they'd seen angels and one of the angels told them that this child is special. And Mary pondered what they said, because she too has had a visit from an angel.

The boy grew up, learned a trade – in an undistinguished time, and in an undistinguished place. He had a flair for storytelling, and loved visiting nearby towns. He spent his days with people his mother and father would prefer he avoid. It was a time of foreign occupation, and his stories and teachings ultimately got him into trouble and so the authorities did away with him. His young adulthood ended abruptly. He was executed as a criminal. His life had been interesting to a few – but no one of any real influence. There were stories about a resurrection – but the first witnesses – apostles they came to be called – were mostly women – and so the stories were ignored by most. Yet, in the generations that followed, more and more came to experience the wisdom in these stories – and the power of this man's presence or Spirit – who believers said was present even after his death – even today.

The teachings of this man Jesus were mostly about honoring lowliness and shedding the things that smother us, about losing our attachments to the things of this world, about beginning to live in a new way. Some of Jesus' sayings that capture it best are: "… many who are first will be last, and the last will be first." *(Matthew 19:30);* and "… the least among all of you is the greatest." *(Luke 9:48)*; "The greatest among you will be your servant." *(Matthew 23:11)*; "Whoever becomes humble like a child is the greatest in the kingdom of heaven." *(Matthew 18:4)*.

And the stories that are attributed to him are stories that just don't fit in the charmed lives that most of us strive for – like the story of the landowner, who represents God, who pays all his workers the same wage at the end of the day, whether they've worked all day or just one hour! (*See Matthew 20:1-16*) These ideas got Jesus killed – because they're dangerous. They upset the way our world works. They honor lowliness and expose the pointlessness of superiority. They call us to avoid any and all behavior that builds us up at the expense of others – and they urge us to serve others – even though it may be at our own expense. The message of God in Jesus is one that is addressed to the lowly – not to the superior. It's a message that makes sense to women who are sold as chattel, or to people who live in refugee camps – or to people who are agonizing over the loss of a loved one. But it is a message that is out of sync with many of our most treasured values. Lowliness is neither fashionable nor attractive – and yet it is where God lives. Weakness is a thing to avoid – and yet it is precisely the characteristic that God most understands and can use. Being vulnerable is neither fun nor chic – and yet it is the mode of being in which God is most likely to interact with us. It's what all this church stuff is about – it's what Christmas is about: interacting with God – moving in a living relationship with God so that in the strength of that relationship we can live in ways that transform the world. And the first step in that process is to come into the experience of our lowliness – to come into the experience of God's lowliness – in the company of a baby with no social credentials – and a pedigree that's sketchy at best – to acknowledge what is weak and broken in our lives and discover God is there waiting for us.

However we imagine or understand God to be, however we organize our sacred trappings, none of it matters until we experience God. Relationship with God is not the conclusion of an argument, or an orderly affair that we can conjure up by singing a familiar hymn – but rather it is a mode of experience.[1] And that experience is often messy, because God is most apt to meet us in the weakest and most vulnerable aspects of our lives.

To those who are enjoying success in your careers at this moment – Congratulations! Share your success with others. To those whose

---

[1] This notion is best expressed by William Temple in his book, *Christus Veritas* (London: Macmillan and Co., 1939), see chapter III, "Religious Experience," pages 35-46.

marriages are strong and healthy at the moment – Congratulations! Offer your strength of relationship to others.   To those who are without weakness, without brokenness, and unwilling, or unable to be vulnerable – God is patient. Try again at Easter. For the rest of us: may our familiar Christmas story shake us into a new awareness that within the majesty, glory, and mystery of Almighty God, there is an intimate experience of God being offered us again this evening. God is *not* too busy. God is *not* disinterested. God is available in the details of our lives, even the ones that may seem puny, in ways and moments that are deeply personal. As we can lose our attachments to the things that make us great – even secure – as we can embrace and experience our own lowliness – we may be posturing ourselves to be renewed in our relationship and experience of the living God. Almighty God lives with us in our lowliness. God is available to you and me – *again*. God is available. *Amen.*

EPIPHANY

Fig Tree Time

Season of Epiphany – Patricia R. Davis

Nathanael asked him, "Where did you get to know me?" Jesus answered, "I saw you under the fig tree …"   John 1:48

Our daughter Genevieve has inherited my love of trees. I grew up on an island outside of Savannah, in a house surrounded by great old trees, just a very short walk from the river. My parents' house is bordered on the front by five or six ancient oak trees, whose branches reach across the road to join those on the other side, forming an arbor of deep shade. The oaks are heavy with Spanish moss, and there is a peace there that is unlike anyplace else I've ever been … being there does something for my soul that nothing else can do. I'm fond of saying that my blood pressure drops ten points just driving over the bridge to home. So I wasn't surprised when our daughter took to the trees when she became a teenager. In our yard here we have a huge magnolia, which she loved to climb and which became, in middle school, a haven, a place of solitude and renewal. To it she would take all of her frustrations with her parents and all of her fears about not fitting in. In its branches, she could find respite from a world that seemed too big and too much. She would take her favorite book of the moment and climb up into its branches, to sit there for hours reading among the birds and squirrels who made it their home. I suspect she knew in some place deep inside that it was a place where she might meet God.

So when I read the lessons for this morning, the thing that was immediately interesting to me was the fig tree. What in the world was Nathanael doing under a fig tree? I discovered that the fig tree is prized in the Middle East for its generous shade and its prolific fruit. The figs are easily dried and so they make a good food for travelers. The fig also has medicinal properties as a poultice applied to wounds and boils. And it was common in those times for men to gather under the shade of the fig tree to study the scriptures in a spot sheltered from the hot sun. So this isn't a miracle story in which Jesus "sees" Nathanael in some kind of vision – Jesus, as he was walking down the road, really did see him a distance away, under a fig tree.

The fig tree was a common meeting place but it appears that on this day Nathanael was by himself and I wondered why. Where was everyone else? But we know where they were: they were out there earning a living, running errands, taking care of the family, going to meetings! And I got to thinking about how difficult it is to carve out time to read, to study, to pray, to spend time hashing out life's mysteries with friends. That kind of time seems so rare nowadays. We were telling our youngest, Margaret, when she was home from college recently that this is the only time in your life when you can read all you want, choose the things you want to study, spend quality time with friends and someone else pays for it! It doesn't get much better than that!

But my own days seem like a succession of tasks, one after the other, that absolutely swallows time and leaves me, at the end of the day, with little left over in time or energy. My prayers often seem to consist of moments in the car on my way to work or a desperately spoken "Help me, Lord" as I approach yet another nursing home resident. I confess that getting meals, skimpy as they are, or doing laundry or reading the newspaper, all can take precedence over the quiet time that I know I need. And if this is the case for those of us who are supposed to put the spiritual life first, how much harder is it for people with jobs in the *real* world?

I'll tell you a painful truth. The long walks I used to take under the trees in Savannah are now only an annual event, but, really, I haven't looked very far to find someplace here that holds that kind of spiritual mystery for me. I don't go looking for a symbolic fig tree, or magnolia or oak very often. And I don't do it for two reasons, okay, maybe three. First, I'm afraid that if I spend time by myself, God won't have anything to say to me. Silence can be a pregnant thing, full of possibilities or it can be mighty empty and boring and scary. It's the terror of every sermon preparation time – that time when I sit with the lessons in front of me and wait for God to say something. It's actually a struggle of wills as I fight the urge to get busy and put something down on paper, and instead, just stay still long enough for God to approach. What if God isn't talking to me this week? It's always a struggle to sit and wait.

Second, I'm afraid that if I spend time alone and be quiet, God might actually speak! What if, God help us, God actually has something to say? What if God actually sees me sitting under that figurative tree and comes near? He might actually call me by name, as he did Samuel, in the heavy silence of the night; he might see me sitting there and have need of me. It's happened before and I said (sort of), "Speak, Lord, for your servant is listening," and look where it got me! God actually might have something to say, again, and then I would have to do something – and it might not be something I want to do! And then I would have to remember that I'm not really in charge… As Paul said in Corinthians, "You are not your own…" I'd have to stop thinking this is something I'm doing!

And third, I might have to look at some things that I don't want to look at. When we spend time alone, a lot of thoughts and feelings can come bubbling to the surface that would be more comfortably left buried. I might have to look at the fact that my relationship with God has been one in which I often take him for granted, in which I sometimes fail to invest myself. I might have to acknowledge the wounded, unhealed and unrepentant parts of myself that I cling to as parts of my identity. I might have to make some painful changes.

The truth is, we can find lots of reasons not to sit under the fig tree. Finding "alone-time" really is a matter of choice. We can be as busy and as distracted as we choose to be. As it says on a magnet on my refrigerator, "Please don't tell me to relax; it's only my tension that's holding me together." There is something in us that likes being busy. It makes us feel useful, productive, even… maybe?… important! We can complain about how busy we are and there's a certain status in that. Why, we're so busy holding the world together, what would happen if we actually let go and sat under a fig tree waiting for God?

Well, we might find that fig tree time still has medicinal properties. It just might be that time spent waiting for God is time for rest and healing. It might just be time in which we tend to those hurts we've been shielding so long, so that they have a chance to heal and we have a chance to get stronger. It might be that fig tree time will give us the opportunity to look around, to notice the shade God so thoughtfully provides for our souls. It might be a time when we discover that there are other people, sitting in the dirt under the fig tree, asking the same questions. We might not be so alone after all.

We might also find that our symbolic fig tree still bears fruit for us in our day too. It may just be that time we spend waiting in the shade for the Lord to come down the road provides us with nourishment for the journey. It may just give us a store of spiritual food to see us through the days when the sun is hot and there isn't any shade. And we may just find that out of the glare of our busy, busy lives, it's quiet enough and peaceful enough to hear the sound of footsteps coming down the road, and we're finally rested enough and ready enough to "come and see."

God's Special People?

Season of Epiphany – John J. Capellaro

Then Peter began to speak to them: "I truly understand that God shows no partiality, but in every nation anyone who fears him and does what is right is acceptable to him."
Acts 10:34-35

We are here to celebrate. And by "*we*," I don't mean just us. When we come together to pray and receive communion; when we are baptized; when we accept forgiveness; whenever we say YES to God, we join in a cosmic celebration: a celebration that's marked by surprise, radical freedom, and an absence of fear. The hallmarks of saying YES to God are almost always surprise, radical freedom, and the absence of fear.

As we read through the gospel of Mark, we can feel the surprise, freedom, and absence of fear that motivates every sentence in Mark's acclamations about Jesus. Mark presents Jesus wrapped in the familiar verses of Hebrew Scripture as he describes the scene of his baptism: "the heavens were torn apart," "A voice came from heaven …" and "You are my Son." Verses borrowed from Ezekiel, the Psalms, and Isaiah all help the listener recognize Jesus as a messianic figure. But then as we come to some level of trust in this main character of Mark's story, we are surprised to discover that there are striking contradictions. Jesus is a man who makes no kingly entrance. Jesus comes from Galilee – an area surrounded by Hellenistic cities and populated mostly by Gentiles – and consequently an area regarded with either suspicion or contempt by most Jews of any standing. The King that Mark presents is a man of dubious social origins who needs ritual cleansing in Baptism, just like anyone else. If God's new day is dawning in Jesus, it is a new age like no one expected. And the thing that's most surprising in Mark's presentation of Jesus is that this Jewish Messiah comes not just for Jews. He comes for all people. Apparently God isn't as interested in special people as many thought. Perhaps we Christians aren't as special as *we* sometimes think. And alongside the surprise of a messiah this open – is the freedom and absence of fear for many of us to consider, "Maybe I am included too."

Our Season of Epiphany that began last Thursday with the story of the Magi visiting the Christ presents us with a Messiah who is being revealed to the world – not just to the chosen people of God. Astrologers from another culture honor Jesus as a King. These are not people who worship the One True God – and yet it is these outsiders whom God leads to the Christ; it is these magicians, sorcerers, if you will, whom our faith tradition holds onto as somehow important for us to remember. Christ is made manifest to the Gentiles. That's what we're dealing with in the season of Epiphany. The idea that God's plan includes all people, perhaps even all life, is received by many with an expression of, "You've got to be kidding!" – in other words, an Epiphany.

The more time I spend with Scripture, the more I listen to people's wonderfully varied experiences of God, Christian and non-Christian, the more I'm around people in their final days of life, the more I reflect on the sacrifice that Jesus offered of his own life, the more I have come to believe that Christ really is for the world. PERIOD. That's my Epiphany. I think that's what Peter was talking about in our lesson from Acts today. He had mellowed from his former days as a rule follower – and is beginning to discover the radical freedom in saying *yes* to God in Christ. Then Peter began to speak to them: "I truly understand that God shows no partiality, but in every nation (Babylon, Persia, Syria, worlds unknown) – anyone who fears him and does what is right is acceptable to him." Jesus Christ – he is Lord of all. That's Peter's Epiphany. And that is a surprise that produces freedom and eliminates fear.

All the stuff we've been handed by "Church" about having to meet this criteria or that in order to be in God's favor – or say this or say that – or do this or so that – or worst of all, "believe this or believe that," in order to get into heaven – is, I believe, nonsense.

Salvation, forgiveness, judgment is all God's to give – and ours to receive. If Jesus' life has any value, it is to show us that God's judgment is to serve Creation and offer radical, unbridled mercy. How many of the Apostles were Baptized? How many signed a statement of faith? How many recited a Creed? How many saw Jesus crucified and still weren't sure who he was? This is not about being in a special private club of the saved. God doesn't work well in private clubs. The Epiphany insists that we accept the impossible: somehow all life is precious to God, and none of it will be lost.

What Church can offer is a community of people who have had a sufficient taste of God through Christ to make a commitment to stay in community – serving each other, out of Christ's love, learning to grow in our faith together, knowing that we'll never have all the answers, pledging to leave judgment to God and saying our prayers in awe that we are loved at all – let alone loved so fully as to be gifted with Christ and one another. The rites of the Church are our saying *yes* to God through Christ. Baptism, in particular is our acknowledgment that in Christ, God has acted for all life – for the entire world – baptized or not – Christian or not – Gentile and Jew – even pagan astrologers from the East.

I think as we slap the palms of our hands to our foreheads and say "AHA," and revel in the radical freedom of accepting all persons, of respecting the dignity of every human being – in that moment of receiving the Holy Spirit – there's a celebration – and not just in this church. I think there's a celebration in the heavens with the angels and archangels, and with all the saints in Light. I think in that Epiphany moment – in that moment when God's Spirit rains in on us, if we had eyes, I think we'd see the heavens torn apart, and there would be God, the angels, archangels, and all the Saints, millions of souls, simultaneously raising their hands in the air, with tears of joy streaming down billions of faces, and a chorus of voices saying, "Yes! They get it! Another Epiphany! Yes! Celebrate! All Life! Celebrate! God shows no partiality. Jesus Christ is Lord of all! Alleluia! Jesus Christ is Lord of all! Alleluia!" *Amen.*

Life, Interrupted

Season of Epiphany – Patricia R. Davis

When the wine gave out, the mother of Jesus said to him, "They have no wine." And Jesus said to her, "Woman, what concern is that to you and to me? My hour has not yet come." John 2:3-4

As much as I hate to admit it, sometimes I'm just not paying attention. Oh, I think I am. I can even be paying particularly close attention but, still, I'm not paying attention. Because something will happen that brings me up short and I realize that what's been going on isn't what's really going on at all. Let me give you an example. Not too long ago I was making visits in the nursing home. Now some of the residents are very sick and I find my time with them is very intense as I try to meet their needs. So this morning in particular, I was really concentrating on listening to an older woman. Over a period of about 20 minutes, as we visited together, her aide was in and out several times. While she never really interrupted, I was aware of her coming and going. It was distracting. I was trying to conduct a pastoral call here. And as I was leaving, she came in again. *Thank you,* she said, *for spending time with Mary. I really appreciate it.* Well, I did what I usually do; I made nice noises. *Thank you very much. I'm glad I can help.* You know, the kinds of things you were raised to say when someone says something kind. *No, wait a minute,* she said. *Listen! I really am glad you're here. Because when I see you, then I remember that God is in this place.* She took my breath away. She had summed up in one sentence my reason for being ordained. She told me why I had come to work that day. She brought God out in the open and made him known.

I tell you this story not out of any pride, but out of thanksgiving and

44

awe, because I am continually amazed that what I think I am doing and what is really happening are such different things. What I thought I was doing was visiting a sick resident. What I was really doing was shoring up the spirit of a staff member.

It's not unlike this story from the Gospel of John. Jesus has come to Cana as a wedding guest. His ministry is newly underway and he has just begun to gather around him a group of people who share his vision. But for now, he's part of the celebration. And that isn't a small responsibility. In his day, no wedding invitations were sent out because the entire community was expected to attend the festivities, which extended over several days. A wedding was not a family affair but one in which the whole community had a stake. And then, as now, a centerpiece of the Jewish wedding was the thanksgiving over the wine. It's one of 7 prayers that witness to God's sustaining grace through life. As the bride and groom drink from the cup of wine, the rabbi prays, *Blessed art Thou, Lord our God, ruler of the universe, who created the fruit of the vine.* He goes on to say, *As you have shared the wine from this cup, so may you, under God's guidance, draw contentment, comfort, and felicity from the cup of life. May you find life's joys heightened, its bitterness sweetened, and all things hallowed by true companionship and love.* The wine is symbolic of God's blessing and the sharing in the wine symbolizes the community's vow to help bring about those blessings.

So Jesus was there as a member of the community, but his mother interrupted him with a request that he do something about the sudden lack of wine. But Jesus just wants to be there as a guest, just for once to simply be and not have to *do* one more thing. For once, let his being part of the party be enough. He must have wondered if there wasn't *any* time when he could stop problem solving, when he could be off duty. He'd like to take a break from this claim of God's on his life. But we can almost hear his mother say, *Wait a minute! Listen! I'm glad you're here.* Because we know from what he did that he was called out of his role as guest and called into making God known. It was in the interruption that Jesus heard his call. In the interruption he became God's icon. In the interruption …

But oh, it's so hard to be interrupted. To go in to work with a list of people to see and things to do and, at the end of the day, to find that we've only gotten through half of it. To begin the day with grand plans and then to get to the end of it and find not one of them was fulfilled. If we measure success by how many items we can tick off the list, we come home a discouraged people most days. Because we can get caught up in our accomplishments; we can make these "the idols that can not speak" which Paul wrote about in his letter to the Corinthians. We make idols of the many tasks we get done. How many phone calls are returned or errands run or meetings attended or household chores done. But, then, if the day includes numerous interruptions, we can end up feeling frustrated and angry – unless we know that there is meaning in the interruptions.

Because our religion, if it is to be any use at all, is a practical thing. It's not meant to be hung up in the coat closet, worn only on Sunday mornings and then shut away again until the next week. And faith, if it is any use at all, is a living thing, which interrupts our lives constantly with its demands for an altered attention.   An attention to the interruptions as times where God may be found ... those moments in which our real reason for being is revealed. As my real reason for being at the nursing home is often to symbolize God's pervasive presence, and as Jesus' real reason for being at the wedding was to demonstrate the extravagant generosity of the God who *is* love, so all of us have moments when God interrupts us with a splash of water in the face. And the real reason becomes clear. Suddenly we know that what we are doing in any particular place and time isn't what we assumed but something else entirely.

Time for one more story. A couple of weeks before Christmas, I went to a local department store to pick up 200 shopping bags donated for us to use at the nursing home to deliver gifts to the residents. I had just finished doing some shopping for them and I was feeling pushed for time, anxious to get back. There were still several residents I needed to see before I went home that day. I was met by a man in Customer Service who said, *I've got them all ready for you but they're back in the warehouse.* Oh, great! So I went with him up escalators, through the aisles, back into the depths of the store. And as we walked along together he began to tell me how difficult Christmas was for him, how it brought back bad memories. He had even tried to commit suicide one Christmas. Now he was dealing with his annual depression by helping others through their holiday. In telling me his story, he interrupted what should have been a simple, straightforward errand and, thank God, this time I was paying attention! This time I knew why I was there, doing what I was doing.

This is the challenge for us in the story of water turned to wine. We are challenged to pay attention and to see the world's need as God sees it. We are challenged to let go of our plans long enough to participate in God's plan. We are challenged to see in the interruptions of child and phone and co-worker and stranger, the hand of God. In this challenge is one of God's best promises: that He will turn *us* from water into wine for someone who needs it just then. *Amen*

Forgiven and Healed

Season of Epiphany – John J. Capellaro

Then some people came, bringing to Jesus a paralyzed man, carried by four of them. And when they could not bring him to Jesus because of the crowd, they removed the roof above him; and after having dug through it, they let down the mat on which the paralytic lay. Mark 2:3-4

The view is magnificent from the home that is believed to be that of Peter. The roof to the house is gone, but the walls remain, and it sits on the edge of Lake Gennesaret – also known as the Sea of Galilee, in the town of Capernaum. There's a Roman Catholic chapel that's been built over the top of the original home, and the site attracts thousands of tourists a year. You can just imagine a meal being prepared here and people peering out of the tiny windows of this stone house onto the Lake. You can picture the gatherings of disciples that took place here following our Lord's death, sharing the sacred meal in the incredibly small rooms. It's easy to imagine Peter making his way up the small staircase on the side of the house to maintain the stick and earthen roof.

The ruins of the synagogue immediately next door to Peter's home are sufficiently preserved so that you can still see where people offered sacrifice, where they listened to the Sacred Scriptures being read, where the Rabbis stood to preach, and where the community gathered for their special feasts. This was Peter's synagogue. It is not only likely, but nearly certain that Jesus taught in this very building. You can walk on the same stones that he did; lean on the same walls; see the same hills and sights, smell the same strong smell of fish coming off this ancient Lake that he did.

When Jesus came to Capernaum it is likely that Peter's home became his home. And so when we read today about Jesus retreating to his home in Capernaum, he may well have retreated to this very house that still stands today. Perhaps this is even the very home described in our story today: the home that people crowded into and around in order to hear Jesus teach.

Joshua loved writing and was even a bit of a poet. He'd first learned to read Hebrew by studying Torah, but as he grew into his teens, Joshua discovered other great works and was soon reading in both Hebrew and Greek. Joshua's father had always hoped his son would join him in the family business, but Joshua never seemed too excited about fishing or working with his father. Their relationship was a stormy one. It seemed to Joshua that he never quite measured up in his father's eyes; it seemed to Joshua's father that he could never do anything right for his son. They often said cruel things to each other and their stormy relationship took its toll with the rest of the family. That stormy relationship somehow fit their surroundings. Joshua and his family lived on the shores of Lake Gennesaret, also known as the Sea of Galilee, a twelve mile-long, heart shaped lake – which provided many unpredictable storms of its own.

It was during one of those storms, when Joshua was working on one of his father's boats, that the injury occurred. The wind tossed the boat so severely, that Joshua was thrown across the deck, where his back collided into a huge crate and Joshua was left paralyzed from the waist down. His father's hopes of his son taking over his business died. Joshua's hopes of becoming a renowned traveling poet and teacher also died. The family's life began to deteriorate. There was little help from their synagogue, where the prevailing wisdom was that this accident must be God's punishment for Joshua's sins. The family stopped going to synagogue, and now the faith that had brought them through so much was of no use. The Jewish teachings in which this family had been grounded – which were among the first words that Joshua ever read – no longer had a place in their life. Bitterness crept into their home like a disease.

Rumors of another Jewish teacher named Jesus had begun to circulate throughout Capernaum, especially since one of their neighbors and a fellow fisherman, Simon, had become one of his followers – or Peter as he now liked to be called. The whole town had been talking about how Simon had left a good business to follow this man. But there was also talk about how this teacher, Jesus, was a healer – that many had been cured of diseases. Joshua wondered if this Jesus could cure him. But then that good old common sense that lives so well in the company of bitterness took hold, and he quickly dismissed such childish thoughts.

Tomorrow would be Sabbath, and so kitchens throughout Capernaum were busy preparing the meal for the next day. The men had come home early that afternoon, with good catches from the night before. Joshua, his father, his mother and his two sisters were all in the house together, when Joshua's old friend, Daniel burst in as if the house were on fire. "C'mon, Joshua. You know that Jesus – that ol' Simon went off with? Well he's here in Capernaum – over at Simon's house. We're all going over. C'mon, we'll take you." Joshua's father spoke first: "Daniel, you leave this house at once. We'll have no talk of Jewish teachers or healings. We've suffered enough. Now leave us alone!" Daniel persisted. "Please sir. Let us try. What harm could come of it?" Before Joshua's father could respond, four more of Joshua's friends entered the house. "Is it okay?" one of them asked.

Before Joshua's father could get in a word, Joshua's mother had come out of the kitchen, looked at her husband without saying a word – and her husband's next objection stayed frozen in his mouth. He looked at the floor with disgust, waved his hand with a gesture of dismissal, and left the room. Joshua's mother gave a nod of approval to Joshua's friends, and they quickly lifted Joshua onto an old mattress they'd brought along with handles on the corners. They carried him out of the house on the make-shift litter and ran with him towards Simon's house. Joshua's sisters quickly tore off their aprons and followed.

When they arrived at the home of Simon – now called Peter – there were so many people at the house that they thought perhaps the synagogue next door was starting Sabbath early – but no, all the people were crowded around Simon's house. There was no way they'd get in to see Jesus with all these people. Daniel and the others were already exhausted from hauling their friend on this mattress. Joshua looked up and seeing the crowds said, "Please Daniel. Take me home. This is stupid. I don't want to see this Jesus; I don't want everybody seeing me either. Please take me home."

Just then Joshua's sisters arrived and, seeing the crowds, looked disappointed. Daniel seemed determined. "I know," Daniel said. "C'mon everyone. Follow me." Daniel grabbed one corner of the mattress, and started around to the side of Simon's house. He made his way with his helpers up the stairs on the side of the house to the roof. They laid the mattress down onto the roof and began to survey the sticks that were laid between the beams to find an easy place to dig. Joshua protested, "What are you fools doing? This isn't your home! Stop this now!" As Daniel carefully removed the first large stick from the roof he could see there was considerable digging left to do before they'd be able to create a large enough opening to see in, let alone lower Joshua into the house. As he continued to dig along with the help of his friends, Daniel ignored Joshua's protests, but he couldn't ignore the new helper he had in his work. It was Joshua's father. His father had arrived, quickly figured out what Daniel was doing, and was now furiously ripping away sticks and earth alongside Daniel. As the hole began to open, Joshua's father started tearing his robe and shirt into strips of cloth and attaching them to the mattress handles. In minutes they'd opened an enormous hole in Simon's roof and were lowering a now silent and stunned Joshua into the center of Simon's house. As they did, the person speaking stopped mid- sentence, and looked up just in time to be blessed with a mouthful of falling dirt and debris. It was Jesus!

Even though they'd never seen him before they knew this was the one everyone had been talking about. Jesus stood up, spit out the dirt, and laughed out loud! He laughed so hard that a silence came over everyone in the house. As the mattress settled onto the floor, Jesus looked at Joshua, smiled, and said, "Son, your sins are forgiven." He then looked up at Joshua's father, who was hanging over the edge of the hole and said to him, "And so are yours!" The silence continued to ring in everyone's ears, and perceiving that some of the religious types were a bit unsettled by his proclamation of forgiveness, Jesus turned to the Scribes and asked them, "Which is easier, to say to this young man, 'Your sins are forgiven,' or to say 'Stand up and take your mat and walk?' So that you may know that these things are the same – and that the one who speaks has the authority to forgive, I say ..." and Jesus turned back to Joshua, leaned down and took Joshua's hand, and said, "Stand up; take up your mat and go home." Joshua, still stunned from all that had brought him here, obediently stood up, picked up a corner of the mattress, and began to make his way to the door. The still silenced crowd opened a pathway for Joshua, and as they did, Jesus could feel a drop of water land on his face. He looked up and saw Joshua's father hanging over the edge of the hole, with tears falling like rain. The only sound you could hear above the whispers of amazement was that of Jesus laughing.

Healing and forgiveness hinge on one another. Don't ever let the church or priests or anyone else stand in the way of the forgiveness offered by God in Christ. Tear through whatever roofs you need to in order to receive his blessing. Trust in the power of forgiveness that is God's to offer, and revel in the wholeness that comes from reconciliation with God through Christ. *Amen.*

Lifted Up by Love

Season of Epiphany – Patricia R. Davis

Now Simon's mother-in-law was in bed with a fever, and they told Jesus about her at once. He came and took her by the hand and lifted her up. Then the fever left her, and she began to serve them. Mark 1:30-31

When I was growing up, my Dad wouldn't let us watch those miracle evangelists on TV. You know the ones I'm talking about – they'd slap people on the forehead and yell at them and suddenly the sick people were healed! These evangelists were fascinating ... and troubling. I mean, I know there were miracle cures in the Bible, but really, it's pretty hard to accept that kind of healing nowadays, and pretty hard to find it, too.

Just recently we held a memorial service in the nursing home for residents who had died in the last month. Among them were some people I had grown very fond of, people who had encouraged me on my journey, people who still had things to do, who were much too glad to be living to die. There were 35 names on that list and every one of them was not cured. Oh, I can give you all sorts of terrific theological arguments about why and how people are suddenly healed but none of them holds much water when it comes to real people and real life and why those I love don't get healed. So when I hear some story about Jesus coming in and healing Simon's mother-in-law and then healing everyone in town, I want to know why wasn't he there when my friends died? Maybe it's just that miracles happened then, but they don't anymore... Or maybe they had more faith then? That's a popular idea, that you just have to have faith to be healed. But that seems to me just another way of blaming the victim, not exactly what a sick person needs. But maybe if Mark had told us more, like what were their illnesses and what did Jesus say and do exactly, and exactly how they were healed...maybe if we had that information, we could unlock this mystery and we wouldn't feel so lost and afraid when our bodies start to fail.

But the Bible, much as we would wish it, isn't a how-to book. It's more a book about a relationship and what that relationship is like, so I'm afraid we have to look at it differently if we're to understand something about the healing stories. What you will discover by the end of this sermon is that, as Christians, we still don't know a whole lot about curing, but we do know a lot about healing. The difference is a crucial one. Curing is about restoring the human body to its original state, without disease. One may be cured of cancer or pneumonia or depression … and it may be a miracle because miracles do happen... but the cure may or may not be a part of healing. Healing, on the other hand, is about making someone whole and healing often takes place without a cure. Now Jesus certainly did a lot of curing, but I believe it was healing that he was most interested in. So we will have to resign ourselves to the knowledge that curing will always be something of a mystery to us. But healing … healing we can learn something about. We can, I believe, even be a part of another's healing. And we do have some information about how Jesus healed.

Mark relates that when Jesus entered the house he came and took Simon's mother-in-law by the hand and lifted her up. He took her by the hand and he lifted her up. This way of healing is everywhere; this way of healing is something we've seen. We've seen someone taken by the hand and lifted up and suddenly they were well again. It's just that we don't often know that this is what we've seen.

In the nursing home where I work, there is a woman who is beautiful. Oh, she's probably not much to look at, but she has a porcelain complexion and warm, soft blue eyes and she loves to dance and she's beautiful. Her husband comes in to visit every day and takes her to sit in the sunshine, where they sit close together and whisper sweet nothings. Of course, she can't talk very well because of a stroke but that doesn't seem to hinder their obvious love for each other, a love that has spanned more than 56 years. Last week she was in bed, not feeling well, when he came in. I happened to be passing her room as he went in, and I saw him bend over her bed and kiss her so sweetly and so gently ... This husband knows about healing. See, in his own way, he took her by the hand and lifted her up.

Healing stories are really stories about being personally touched by the saving grace of Jesus. And that kind of healing is still with us, alive, generous, everywhere, all the time. This healing is God's way of calling us to a relationship with him that is beyond the human life span, beyond pain and fear, beyond everything we are afraid to lose. This healing is God's way of saying that we matter, and these healing moments are everywhere.

More often than not, I am the recipient of this healing touch of Jesus. And it never fails to surprise me. Recently I went to wish goodbye and Godspeed to a man who has been in the nursing home for care while he endured radiation treatment for a dangerous cancer. He's a man of immense good humor, but also a pain in the neck to the administration, forever pushing for more care, more thoughtfulness, more of anything and everything for himself and others. We've talked quite a lot and I'd come to admire his resilience in the face of a very real threat to his life. So I went to say goodbye as he graduated from a real "school of hard knocks." What he said to me was interesting, and brought us both to tears. He said, "You know, I have to thank you. Even though you're a chaplain, you never once pushed me. I don't think we ever really had a conversation about God. I guess I'd say that I'm an agnostic, but when I saw you, I knew that God was doing something good in this place." In him, Jesus took me by the hand and lifted me up. It happens more times than I can count, that God brings his healing touch, that God takes me by the hand, just when I am sure that I have absolutely nothing to give to this world. And that is God's way with all of us.

Because God is always where suffering is to be found. Sometimes that suffering is obvious and painful and physical and sometimes it's profoundly everyday. And while what I want, in the face of so much suffering, is to see God to fix it all, I believe with all my heart that what God wants is to heal it all. Because we are more than a collection of vulnerable body parts. We are the love of God's life, the tug on his heartstrings, the hope of his creation. What God sees is more than the sum of all those parts. There is a bumper sticker that says it effectively: "We are not human beings having a spiritual experience; we are spiritual beings having a human experience." So while I want God to fix the human hurts, for God it's about fixing the spiritual hurts. So sometimes God's healing is also curing, but always God's healing is part of a living relationship with Him. And this is the driving force, the ultimate message, the ultimate point of Jesus' life and ministry and death, that whatever happens ... we matter to God. We matter to God so much that he is healing always and everywhere, in all of life's grievous moments, and to our death and beyond.

Though we often struggle to believe it, this healing ministry of Jesus' has not been confined to the worn pages of some outdated Bible stories. It's a ministry that Jesus passed on to his disciples, and that means us. We are called to be in the world as spiritual beings, as well as human beings ... beings who join in God's healing work. Every Sunday we say thank you for this call as He assures us "in these holy mysteries that we are living members of the Body of [his] Son." And we ask that He will "send us out to do the work [he] has given us to do, to love and serve [him] as faithful witnesses of Christ our Lord." This is nothing less than a plea that his healing work be done in us and through us, as his disciples today. It's the continuing, living story of redemption, that with each of us, and through each of us, in ways that are miraculous and mysterious and as close as breathing, Jesus takes us by the hand and lifts us up and, God willing, we are healed. *Amen.*

God in a Box

Transfiguration Sunday – John J. Capellaro

... Jesus took with him Peter and James and John, and led them up a high mountain apart, by themselves. And he was transfigured before them ... And there appeared to them Elijah with Moses, who were talking with Jesus. Then Peter said to Jesus, "Rabbi, it is good for us to be here; let us make three dwellings, one for you, one for Moses, and one for Elijah." He did not know what to say, for they were terrified. Mark 9:2-6

Today is Transfiguration Sunday. Today we recall the fantastic vision of Peter, James, and John that takes place on a hilltop in Galilee: a vision of Moses, through whom God gives The Law, standing with Elijah, through whom God gives prophecy, taking their place alongside Jesus, through whom God gives salvation. Peter wants to preserve this remarkable scene and build dwellings for these agents of God – to put boxes around the moment and around the people – but God intervenes and speaks to the disciples saying, *"This is my Son; listen to him!"*

A few years ago I had the good fortune of spending two weeks in Israel. I can now say: "Been there. Done that." Yeah, I've visited all the places where Jesus was. Took 432 slides. I can prove I've "been there and done that." Don't you hate that expression? It trivializes whatever it refers to, doesn't it? It implies that our experiences can be put into little boxes without having to reflect further on their relevance in our lives. And yet putting our experiences into little boxes is precisely what many of us do, isn't it? On the plane to Israel I prepared my whole trip so that I could fit every moment into its own neat little box. I made a "been there; done that" list of the places I wanted to see in Israel. Yeah,

I wanna see where Jesus was crucified. I wanna cross the Sea of Galilee. I wanna float in the Dead Sea. Blah, blah, blah. I wanna to take a bunch of slides, capture it all – sort of bring Israel back home in a box.

Many of us put boxes around the events in our lives: we make weddings into Cecil B. Demille productions, as if the event is more important than the life to which it calls us. We tend to compartmentalize our lives: Church is on Sunday; that's where the spiritual stuff happens. Yeah. "Been there. Done that." Work is Monday through Friday; that's where we earn the money. Family – that's a Saturday thing. Sunday becomes one reality, Monday another, and Tuesday yet another. We put boxes around not just our experiences, but around our truths, around people, and around our beliefs. We are often eager to call ourselves conservative or liberal, as if one such label might adequately cover every issue in our lives. Church people are great at putting boxes around things. There are those who enshrine a particular translation of the Bible, style of worship, or ritual practice, so that maturity in the faith and community become secondary.

Then there are those people who love those personality profiles, such as Myers-Briggs, so that they can put boxes around everyone. I'll never forget my first day of seminary, when a classmate approached me and said, "Hi. My name is Susan; I'm an ENFP, what are you?" (*You know Extroverted, Intuiting, Feeling, and Perceiving.*) I looked at her straight in the eye and said, "I'm an LMNOP." She stared at me blankly, as if there were some new method of putting boxes around people she hadn't heard about yet. I'm especially tickled by those moralizing bumper stickers that pretend to solve very complex issues with one sentence of so-called "truth-in-a-box."

I'm not sure why we put people, ideas, and experiences into boxes – but indeed we do just that. And so being no different than anyone else – I began my trip through Israel with my own inventory of boxes to put around each piece of this visit to Israel. One such visit was to the Church of the Holy Sepulcher in Jerusalem. There is good evidence that this was a site where crucifixions were routinely held, and quite possibly the very site where Jesus was crucified. Inside the church are three smaller chapels, one of which is built around the gigantic rock on which these crucifixions likely took place. The Greek Orthodox Church, which maintains this part of the church, has built an enormous glass box around the rock, and on top of the glass-encased rock is an altar. We waited in line for a very long time to reach the altar, which has become one of Israel's most popular tourist attractions. Under the altar there is a ledge covered with an ornate metal plate, which has a hole in it. You can kneel down under the altar, stick your arm into the hole, and actually touch the rock. Thousands of people wait in line to do this each year. Well, I hadn't traveled all the way to Israel to miss being able to say, "Been there; done that." So I waited in line. Finally it was my turn. Conscious of the many people behind me in line, I quickly knelt down, made my way under the altar, and stuck my arm deeply into this hole. I felt the icy cold rock, said a mechanical prayer, and began to move away as quickly as I could. Problem was, I couldn't move. My arm was stuck in the hole. No kidding. Millions of Christian pilgrims go through this ritual at this holy site every year, and I get my arm stuck in the hole. I imagined the news broadcast that evening:

> American tourist has to be removed from ancient Jerusalem shrine with "jaws of life." Man identified as *former* priest in American Episcopal Church.

My praying stopped. I was struck silent and all I could do was smile. As I did, I relaxed. The overwhelming feeling I had was of our Lord, saying: *"Listen to me, John. Just be with me for a moment."* As that feeling took hold, I wept and my arm came free.

From that moment on, I began to enjoy the trip. From that moment on, I began to reflect on the connections of a crucified man from two thousand years ago, and the risen Christ who will not leave me alone. I began to let the journey take me, rather than me take the journey. I still took my pictures, but I probably missed the best ones.

The God that is revealed through Christ will not be checked off some list or be kept in a box, will not be locked up in a Book – even the Bible, will not be isolated to a mere event, will not be captured in a particular style of worship, will not be limited to Sunday mornings; will not be bound to one expression of faith, will not be segregated from the respectable nor the despicable, will not be captured in a sermon or poem, will not be put under glass. God is *the* vital presence in our lives; God is available in real time – in ways that *can be* perceived. All we need do is listen. This isn't a fairy tale. Our deepest longings for intimacy with God are neither frivolous nor ill founded. It's just that God is free to act in ways that defy prediction – and in ways that will almost always surprise. And when we insist on keeping God safely locked up in the familiar – or "over there" at the altar – surprises are far less likely to be perceived. What would church look like – no, more importantly, what would our lives look like – if we actually listened for God with the expectation of hearing God, fully expecting to be touched by God's very real presence, and without limiting that potential experience by our present sense and knowledge? Lent begins this Wednesday. I pray we use this season as a time to practice our listening, and perhaps begin letting God out of the boxes we have so carefully built for *her*. *Amen*.

Just Lay That Burden Down

Season of Epiphany – Patricia R. Davis

*Then some people came, bringing to him a paralyzed man,
carried by four of them. And when they could not bring him to
Jesus because of the crowd, they removed the roof above him; and
after having dug through it, they let down the mat on which the
paralytic lay.* Mark 2:3-4

Our daughter Margaret was home from college recently and I enlisted
her help in sermon writing. "What in the world am I going to say about
these healing stories," I asked her. She thought hard for a minute or so
and then she said, "You can tell them, 'Jesus went around healing people.
That's a good thing. You can't argue with that! ... Y'all come over to the
parish house for a cup of coffee! The mall doesn't open till noon.' "
Well, I have to tell you, I was tempted! There are so many healing
stories all in a row in Mark and it's a struggle to figure out what it is we're
supposed to understand from these miracles. I want to say, "Enough
already, I don't have any more good ideas to preach on!" but Mark will
not let us go, so here we go.

This is among the most famous healing stories, the story of the
paralytic being let down through a hole in the roof. It sounds a strange
thing but it really isn't a story much different from that of lots of people
even today. Here come these friends, two on each end of the litter (they
could be pushing a wheelchair), carrying their friend to a faith healer in
hopes that he'll be cured. We know this behavior. This is the response
of any of us faced with a grim and terrifying diagnosis, the desperate flight
from hope to hope, praying that something will work, something will
make everything all right again. There is a desperation and a hope here

that will go anywhere, do anything, even demolish a neighbor's roof, if it will just make things right.

The friends in this story are right here at St. Paul's. They are the long-suffering among us: the parents up every night for hours on end walking a baby screaming with colic or the children struggling to squeeze in a visit to their aging parents between office deadlines. They are the spouses, fighting to maintain some semblance of a marriage in the face of an illness that changes everything. They are us every time we walk the mile and bear the load for someone else, in the hope of relief and cure. Such behavior is sacrificial, in many ways the fulfillment of Jesus' saying that "Greater love has no man than this, that he lay down his life for his friend." Many of these everyday heroes are doing just that, laying down their lives for someone else, every day, day after day.

We're pretty good about recognizing and honoring that. What we're not good at is recognizing the gift of frustration, of being just plain "fed up"! It's just possible that these friends of the paralytic were just plain fed up with it all. Maybe they had just had enough of helping him to do everything all the time. Maybe they were sick and tired of toting him from doctor to doctor. Maybe this was just the latest and last attempt to find a way to lay their burden down.

When our daughter Genevieve was six and her sister Margaret just newborn, Genevieve was the epitome of the big sister. She sang to Margaret and told her stories and rocked her in the cradle. It was wonderful to see. But after about 2 weeks I knew the thrill was wearing off when I got up one night, hearing Margaret cry. And as I passed Genevieve's room, I heard her roll over in bed and say, "Oh, for Pete's sake!" It spoke volumes about her ability to carry this responsibility of being a big sister and about her need to be relieved of the burden of it. "Oh, for Pete's sake!" – the exclamation of all of us at one time or another when what we carry simply cannot be borne any longer.

I want to suggest that this frustrated, fed-up-to-the-gills feeling is not a curse but a blessing, a little glimpse into the mind of God, who knows when to carry the burden of us and when to put it down. Just look at the Old Testament lesson, Isaiah 43:18-25. Not exactly an example of how wonderfully worthy we are of God's great love – "you have been weary of me, O Israel!" Through Isaiah, God lists all the things he has done and is doing and will do for his people, and then God says, "you have burdened me with your sins, you have wearied me with your iniquities. I blot out your transgressions for my own sake..." He says in effect that he is so fed up with us that he will forgive us, just to give up the burden of it, move on, do something different for a change! Even – I should say especially – God knows when enough is enough!

And it seems to me that these friends of the paralyzed man knew also that enough was enough, because they took him to Jesus, which is where we should go first and where we're all going to end up eventually anyway. And Jesus, seeing the man, and his desperate friends holding the ropes above, cuts right to the heart of the problem and says, "Your sins are forgiven." And it's just possible that Jesus was talking not just to the paralyzed man but to his friends also. Because it can become sin, to carry our load too long, too far, without seeking relief for that burden. It's a seductive trap. Our troubles do have their benefits: we can feel righteous, long-suffering, and oh so worthy of sympathy and praise. Oh, the glory of recounting my aches and pains, the places arthritis has turned up, the hours I spent on that report for the office, the things I gave up to put our kids through college!

But we're reminded in this story that if we're not carrying those burdens to the Lord, we're carrying them in the wrong direction. Just as caregivers need a day off, and alcoholics need AA, and parents need baby-sitters, we all need to attend to our personal limits and the ways in which, because we keep on carrying our burdens indefinitely, we fail to set them down in front of the One who can heal them. I've been there. We all have. And I never thought that as a Deacon, I'd be telling people to think long and hard about acts of ministry, but here it is: When we see a need, we should do something about it, but we must not become so attached to it that we can't let it go, pass it on, or set it down. We must find ways not only to minister but to turn that ministry over to God. If we don't, we run the very real risk of becoming those excessively pride-filled Christians we've all met who are very busy for the Lord but haven't actually talked with him in months!

So how in the world do we imitate these friends who brought their burden to Jesus? If that fed-up, frustrated, end-of-our-rope feeling is actually a giant message from God that says, *Come to me, all you who are weak and heavy laden, and I will give you rest,* how do we do that? How in the world do we take it to God?

One of the ways that has become increasingly helpful to me is to put my body where my mind is. Let me give you an example. During part of my training, I was in a workshop which was so stress-filled and difficult that I found myself absolutely furious by the end of the session. Then, we were asked to spend some time in prayer to close the session. Well, going to God with this much fury was just about the last thing I wanted to do. My hands were knotted up like my stomach and all I could think about was getting out of there, to heck with this program, this call, this everything! I sat there, fists clenched, begging God to do something about this awful experience and my awful anger. And I found that as I prayed that furious, impotent prayer, my hands opened all by themselves and the anger left, taken away ... just taken away by the only one who can truly bear our burdens. So now, when I pray, I deliberately do so with my hands opened, a posture which allows me to lay down and give away all those incredibly heavy paralyzed parts of myself that I've been carrying around. And with open hands, I am free to receive what God returns to me ...

Our posture in prayer is a place to begin, a place where we may show with our bodies how our souls hurt and encounter the God who waits for us, ready to heal. When we lay down the people and things we've been carrying around for so long, God heals them, beginning with us. It's our sins that are forgiven, our paralyzed bodies that rise up. We have only to come and ask to find that in Him all the promises of God find their *Yes* and in us God will do a new thing. *Amen.*

LENT

God's Call to Life

Ash Wednesday – John J. Capellaro

"...we are but dust, and to dust we shall return..."

God is determined to be in relationship with us. God is eager for us to receive the benefit of that relationship – that life-giving stuff we call Love, that is, God's Holy Spirit: that stuff that feeds hope – that stuff that provides us with the courage to forgive – the motivation to care for those in need – the stamina to face another day. But determined though God is, this gift of relationship – of God's Holy Spirit – with all its benefits, will not be forced upon us. God's stance is one of wooing us. God is within a step of us, crouched down on a knee, inviting. We are asked to turn, come face to face with the one *from whom no secrets are hid*, and receive the relationship that changes us.

But we tend to be busy with other matters – preoccupied with things we think important. We have careers to manage – children to raise – bills to pay – Temples to build. Most of us tend to respond to God's invitation with a courteous,

> *"Oh thank you so much for that kind invitation. Yes. I'd love to accept – give me just another few years, till my kids get through college, or I get that promotion, or ..."* [you fill in the blank.]

And yet God remains steadfast, offering the invitation – the gift of God's Spirit – encouraging, hoping, calling us to that life-giving relationship for which we all have a deep longing. For most of us, it's not until the crises of our lives arise that we begin to recognize the invitation. A time of divorce, job loss, health crises – it's then that our hearing improves. It's then that we are more apt to step back from the temples we've built and see them for what they are. It's then that we are more apt to see the benefits of this God-connection: a loving, nourishing connection that will see us through all the crises of this life into a life beyond – a connection that reveals concrete purpose for *this life*. Most of us don't learn to trust until we have nothing left, until our temples crumble. And then we take up the words of the Psalmist,

> *Cast me not away from your presence*
> *and take not your Holy Spirit from me.*

You'd think God might get peeved with us – only saying "Yes," to God's invitation, after we've tried every option *except* God. But for some reason *(I suppose it's that divine Love stuff again)*, God seems to love these moments of ours. These times when our mortality stares us in the face – when we *know* that

> *"...we are but dust, and to dust we shall return..."*

Because it's then that we listen; it's then that those things which separate us from God begin to crumble. The holy season of Lent begins today. Use this time to reflect on the temples of our own making. Use this time to discover God's presence woven through and through the crises of our lives. May we turn as individuals and as a community and see our Lord kneeling before us – wooing us to a new relationship – a relationship riddled with forgiveness and hope. God's invitation stands.

How do we respond?

When God Bent Down

Maundy Thursday – Patricia R. Davis

Then he poured water into a basin and began to wash the disciples' feet and to wipe them with the towel that was tied around him. John 13:5

God had always been an artist on a grand scale. With the vast expanse of interstellar space for a canvas, all his work to date had been *big*, but on this day (though there wasn't even a day yet, or a night) God decided to do something a little smaller, a little more personal. The angels had been clamoring for something that would use their talents, something that they could be involved in. So God set out to paint a masterpiece, but smaller this time, something that would hang in a special place in the living room of the universe and attract notice by its very smallness, its perfection in miniature.

So God painted a world with oceans of azure and aqua and ultramarine and lands of burnt umber and sage and olive green and he made some animals to liven up the landscape… "And there were green alligators and long-necked geese, humpy-back camels and chimpanzees …" But the angels looked at all this and weren't thrilled. *It doesn't look right,* they said. *Are you sure it's finished?* And God thought, too, that the thing looked incomplete, and then he had his greatest inspiration. *I'll make this a mixed media piece of art,* he thought. And God stooped down on the banks of a river and gathered up some mud and clay. He worked it till it was just the right consistency and then he sculpted two people. And then he bent *way* down and kissed them, and it was the kiss of life. And God said, *At last, here are people who can share all that I dream of, people who are kindred spirits.* And God and the people he had made lived

69

together, and it was incredible. They had long conversations in which God shared his dreams and they shared their hopes. Nothing was scary or sad, but it was all joy and lots of laughter. But then the people began to think that there must be something they were missing and they wanted the freedom to explore and find out for themselves instead of always taking God's word for it. So they took off to see what they could find. But then they were afraid, afraid that God would be disappointed or angry with them and they couldn't bear to see him disappointed or angry, so they hid from him. And that evening when God showed up for their usual walk down by the river, they weren't waiting for him like they usually did. And God knew that the time had come to let them go. So God decided to stand a little way off, close enough to be there if they needed him but not so close as to frighten them. But he missed them.

The story of these people is a long, long story with lots of ups and downs. They struggled to make their way without God's help, but every now and then they found that they missed him too. But God didn't want them to be frightened so the times he came quite close were few and far between. There were so many things that frightened the people now. But one time, when they had been slaves of other people for a long, long time and they despaired of ever seeing the freedom they had left home for, God stooped down again. He stooped down and with his great big hands, held back the water so that they could walk safely on dry land to a new country, a place much like that first place, where everything was milk and honey, grass and flowers. And the people knew that God had to have been involved in that one but it was an awfully big thing, holding back the water, and more than a little scary when you thought about it. So they stayed afraid, even though God hoped that in his help they would see how he yearned for the relationship they once had. He would do anything, if only they would talk with him again like they once did. Because he missed them.

God did a lot of bending down, through eons and ages of people, bending down to help them but always careful not to scare them off. But the people (there were lots of them now) had been so long without seeing God's face that they had forgotten what he looked like. They didn't know how to recognize him and they didn't know how to find him, though there were lots of people, "prophets" they called them, who told them how. So the people muddled along ... they came from mud, you see... until God could stand it no longer. His heart was breaking for them. They tried so hard to enjoy their freedom but all it seemed to bring was heartache and he didn't want them to think they were suffering alone. So God decided to do something very unlike what he had done so far. God decided to show himself to them, but in a way that wouldn't frighten them away.

So God bent way down, bent down from heaven and made himself look like one of them. He made himself to *be* one of them, so that they could see that he understood. He even took a human name, Jesus, hoping that when they heard it they would know that God *saves* his people. And he showed them that he wasn't frightening because he kept on bending down, putting himself on eye level with all kinds of people. One time he bent down and wrote in the dirt to save a woman's life. And another time he bent down and made some mud to heal a blind man's eyes. He bent down and touched people who were sick and hurting. He bent down and picked up little children and whispered sweet love songs in their ears. He hoped that when they saw him bending down, they would remember where they came from and how he had been there with them from the very beginning. And with Jesus, people weren't scared any more. And people began to understand, but slowly, because this was so different from the God they thought they knew.

And then a funny thing happened. People forgot about being scared of God because he was big and powerful and got scared of him because he was close and personal. They began to feel like they did when they had just left Egypt, that maybe sticking with what they knew was better than what they didn't know. This kind of love (from God!) was just too much, too frightening, in a different sort of way. So they began to turn away, to go back to the safety and slavery they knew, until Jesus was left with just a handful of people brave enough to risk their freedom. And God bent down, one more time. He took off his clothes and wrapped a towel around his human frame, and bent down till he was *lower* than eye level, as low as it seemed God could go. He bent down and with a bowl of water, washed away the dirt and mud of a hundred dusty roads traveled searching for God. He bent down and washed them clean as the day of their creation and then he looked up. God looked up and in his eyes they could see such love as to make their hearts break wide open. It was the love of a thousand sunsets, the love of every new mother's cry of joy, the love of every husband's tender heart. Yet it was a love we can scarcely imagine. And he said, *Do you see what I am doing? When I go away, you must do this. You must do this over and over until, by bending down, you see the world from my point of view. Wash each other's feet, and keep on washing them, until you know that this is how I love you. Not angry, not fearful, not ready to punish you because you are so human, but love. Only love. Only love.*

Amen.

Child Sacrifice

Season of Lent – John J. Capellaro

After these things God tested Abraham. He said to him, "Abraham!" And he said, "Here I am." He said, "Take your son, your only son Isaac, whom you love, and go to the land of Moriah, and offer him there as a burnt offering on one of the mountains that I shall show you." So Abraham rose early in the morning, saddled his donkey, and took two of his young men with him, and his son Isaac.   Genesis 22:1-3

Let us pray.

O God, you have taught us through your blessed Son that whoever receives a little child in the name of Christ receives Christ himself: We give you thanks for the blessing you have bestowed upon these families in giving them children. Confirm their joy by a lively sense of your presence with them, and give them calm strength and patient wisdom as they seek to bring their children to love all that is true and noble, just and pure, lovable and gracious, excellent and admirable, following the example of our Lord and Savior, Jesus Christ. Amen.

That's the prayer that we will pray in a few minutes with two families who have been blessed recently with the birth of children. It's a beautiful prayer because it reminds us parents of our need for calm strength and patient wisdom, and it suggests what we might hope for, for our children. There are no requests for our children getting into the right schools, or that they might earn a good living, but rather that they grow up to love all that is true, noble, just, pure, lovable, gracious, excellent and admirable, following the example of Jesus. How many of us structure our lives or our marriages so as to encourage those ideals in our children? How many of us put aside our own self-serving ambitions sufficiently to nourish those hopes for our children?

Sarah and Abraham had a marriage about as healthy as anyone's, I guess. Once when Abraham and Sarah entered Egypt, Abraham said to his wife, whom he loved, *"I know well that you are a woman beautiful in appearance; and when the Egyptians see you, they will say, 'This is his wife;' then they will kill me, but they will let you live. Say you are my sister, so that it may go well with me ... and that my life may be spared."*
From that day on their marriage was more human than heavenly. When Sarah's inability to bear children was acknowledged as a problem, Sarah suggested that Abraham attempt to bring a child into the world with Sarah's servant, Hagar. Abraham obliged Sarah's request – Whatta guy! And a child was born to them. But as is always the case with an event that violates a sacred union, tensions arose, and Sarah's jealousy of Hagar nearly broke the marriage apart. From then on, Abraham and Sarah's marriage would carry a burden – and their skill as parents would reveal a little damage. Some number of years into their marriage God made a promise to Abraham and Sarah to bless them with a child of their own. Through this child the nation of Israel would come to be and flourish. And Abraham fell on his face and laughed out loud at God, because he was ninety-nine years old. When Sarah, who was ninety, heard of the promise, she too laughed out loud, saying, *"At this age, my husband and I shall have pleasure!"* And from that day on, there was a mutual understanding between them that retained some suspicion of God.
But when Abraham turned 100, God did what he had said he would do. Sarah became pregnant and had a son, and they named him Isaac, which means, "He who will laugh." And Sarah said, *"God has brought laughter for me. And everyone who hears will laugh with me."* And the child grew – and their hopes lived. And Abraham's trust in God was strong. And then one day, God tested Abraham. He said, *"Take your son, your only son, Isaac, whom you love, and go to the land of Moriah and offer him there as a burnt offering."* Now Abraham had argued with God before, about how many people God might save from the destruction of Sodom. But today, Abraham doesn't argue with God about

killing his own son. He simply goes to bed, wakes up the next day, saddles his animal, and sets out with his son, Isaac, and two servants – and he doesn't discuss it with Sarah.

When Sarah wakes up, and finds her husband and son gone, she checks with some of the servants, learns that they left early, and were prepared to offer a sacrifice. Perhaps it was time for Abraham to teach their son about prayer and sacrifice. And then she recalls her long history with Abraham. "Was Abraham hearing voices or seeing angels again? Doesn't he yet understand that he cannot know the mind of God?" An intuitive worry sets in. She feels no calm strength, no patient wisdom, just sickness in her stomach. As Abraham makes his way into the wilderness, Isaac becomes increasingly aware of the mystery of this excursion. "Where is our sacrifice, Father?" Abraham simply responds, "God will provide." Abraham doesn't tell Isaac all he wants to know, because he himself does not know. And the two of them walk on – together. Abraham wonders, "Will God make me go through with this? If I kill, do I not make a mockery of God's Law? How can God, who embodies justice – be so unjust? What about God's plan to make my offspring as numerous as the stars? There will be no offspring – no future. Are God's promises for naught? If I sacrifice my son, I sacrifice my faith. *What will I tell Sarah?*"

Isaac – "He who will laugh" – walks with his father. He is old enough to carry wood, to understand sacrifice, and to know his father well. And yet he walks with his father toward God. He walks in that unspeakable peace that can sometimes be found in the company of a parent – coupled with enough experience to know the risks in trusting a parent. Their march continues – the two of them alone now – led by God's unfathomable design. But they are together, of one purpose, albeit unexpressed. They reach the top of the mountain and together they prepare the wood; Isaac is bound and laid upon the altar gazing at his father. Abraham picks up the knife to kill his son, and an angel calls to him to stop. A trembling silence follows. There is a future. But is it as expected?

Abraham returns home with his servants – alone.   And soon after Abraham arrives home, Sarah dies. Isaac would return home also, but not for many years. And he would never be with his father again, in the same way he was, on their way to that mountain. Too much had happened. Isaac the boy, died on that mountain; Isaac, the changed man walked away alone. But he survived, like many other victims of sacrifice; however well intended those sacrifices are, he survived. Isaac, the one who will laugh, became a poet; he married and had children. He did not rebel against life. He devoted his life to the defense of his people. He survived. He made something of his memories and his experience, and in so doing forces us to hope. And I believe he never abandoned the art of laughter. Tradition has it that at the end of time, on that Day of Judgment, Isaac alone will be entitled to say anything he wishes to God – to ask anything of Him – and *not* because he suffered, but because he transformed his suffering into prayer, poetry, love, and laughter. He survived – and survived nobly.

Our survival is linked to his and to the survival of all those who would be sacrificed: all the children who are sacrificed daily to poverty, hunger, AIDS, addiction, inadequate education, violence, and neglect. We are no more whole than Abraham, Sarah, or Isaac. We are at once victim, struggling to remember truth, nobility, justice, poetry and the art of laughter, and the ones holding the knife. But there is hope; survival is possible; and we can find our own poetry in working for all the children who would be sacrificed – and remembering we can survive nobly – even with laughter.

Dear God, bless us with the courage to see how we daily participate in the sacrifice of children and gift us, we pray with calm strength and patient wisdom to bring all children: our own and others – rich and poor – near and far – to love what is true and noble, just and pure, lovable and gracious, excellent and admirable, following the example of our Lord and Savior, Jesus Christ.   *Amen.*

Please Dear God – Give Me a Sign!

Season of Lent – John J. Capellaro

But Moses said to God, "Who am I that I should go to Pharaoh, and bring the Israelites out of Egypt?" He said, "I will be with you; and this shall be the sign for you that it is I who sent you: when you have brought the people out of Egypt, you shall worship God on this mountain." Exodus 3:11-12

Gracious God, give me a sign! Give me a burning bush. Should I take this road or that one? Just give me a sign. Things are falling apart in my marriage. I think it may be finally over. Give me a sign that will tell me what to do. And please let it be what *I* want! I need to change jobs. Give me a sign about what I should do. Give me a burning bush, good Lord! I've been dating this person for over two years now. Should we marry? Give me a sign! Give me a burning bush! I'm thinking about ordained ministry. Is this what you want dear God? Please, give me a sign.

Have you ever found yourself asking for a sign? I've got some good sign stories, and I've heard some good ones too, haven't you? Someone I spoke with recently was telling me that he'd been asking God for a sign, while driving down Virginia Beach Boulevard, and he read something on a billboard that seemed to answer his question. He got his sign – a real sign – and a really big one.

Well today, we get this great sign story from Exodus where Moses is met by a Burning Bush. Now, let's get clear about the sign in this story – or I should say the *signs*, because there's more than one sign being discussed in this reading. In the first part of the story, Moses goes out to Mount Horeb, which translates "wasteland." Mount Horeb is also known as Mount Sinai. So Moses goes out on just another normal day of business *not* looking for any religious experience, just watching the flock. What kind of flock? I don't know. Let's give him goats. Okay? So Moses is out there with his goats; he arrives at the wasteland, Mount Horeb, and suddenly he is distracted by something he sees in a nearby bush. As he approaches the bush, he sees a tongue of fire in the bush, and from this strange sight, Moses hears a voice – and not just any voice. Jewish folklore has it that Moses hears the voice of his earthly father, a voice which reassures him, as it calls him not once – but twice, "Moses, Moses." Then, the voice changes to the voice of God. God begins a dialogue with Moses that calls him to action. "First of all, Moses, show a little manners, and how about taking off those sandals. Since I'm here, this is now Holy Ground." Moses obliges, but it seems that's about as far as Moses wants to go. He's not biting on the rest of this offer.

After God pitches the plan, Moses responds with a clear, "I don't think so, God. I mean it may be a great idea for someone to lead your people out of Egypt and all. But first of all, I don't mind it here in Egypt; secondly, I'm not even known among the Jewish people, and thirdly, this mission you have in mind involves what again? – persuading Pharaoh to let your people leave Egypt, and then, as if that isn't enough, you then thought it might be a good idea for me to lead them across the Sinai into another country – a country that is presently occupied by let's see – I think you said it was the Canaanites, Hittites, Amorites, Perizzites, Hivites, and Jebusites.   Have you heard about those Hittites and Amorites? Now look, it's not that I'm not up for a little traveling. And sure, I enjoy a good battle with some Hittites, Amorites and Jebusites every now and again, just as much as the next guy, *but* you see I've got a wife, and – and – well – this flock here – well – it's not really mine. These goats belong to my father-in-law, and he really expects me to sort of stay with this shepherding thing. So, thanks and all, but I think you have the wrong guy."

And God persists. "Moses, relax. I'll be with you." But Moses is not easily persuaded. "Look God, I really appreciate this sign and all, I mean there have been plenty of times when I have asked you for one – but you know … Who am I to go to Pharaoh? Who am I? And for that matter – who are you? I mean, I know who you are, but if I do this and they ask me who sent me, what am I supposed to tell them?" "Tell them

I AM has sent you." "Come again?" "I AM WHO I AM. You might also think of my name as, 'I am Becoming what I am Becoming.' And if it makes it any easier, I am the God of Abraham, Isaac, and Jacob – and I am also the God of your father, Moses."

Moses stops. "Tell you what, is there any chance you might give me another sign? This tongue of fire is great. Really. But I could really use one more sign – just to be sure." And God said, "... *and this shall be the sign for you that it is I who sent you: when you have brought the people out of Egypt, you shall worship God on this mountain.*" "That's my sign?! You want me to go ahead and do what you ask, and *then* I get my sign? And the sign is me and your people worshiping you here – right where we are now? My sign will be me?"

There may be signs from time to time – signs that reassure us, signs that are instigated by God, that help us know what we need to know. But as often, perhaps more often, we may miss the signs we long for – because we choose not to do them, or *be* them. As we act in trust – we are living signs. Anytime we act in a way that acknowledges God as God, we are becoming a sign from God. Anytime we act in a way that puts someone else before our needs; anytime we forgive the unforgivable; anytime we act in trust that God is God, and we aren't, we become a sign from God.

Let me offer some examples of signs from God that are just as powerful as any burning bush. When we all get up out of our seats and come forward to receive the bread and wine at communion. That's a sign from God. As we well-educated people come up and put out our hands for a piece of squashed bread – in trust – in hope – that Christ is the one through whom we know God – now that's a sign. Or when ... a couple who have been married too long and reach that inevitable place where it seems there may be no reason to continue – where they've become sick and tired of each other's voices – when little habits that were once cute have now become intolerable – when it has become crystal clear that the marriage was a big mistake in the first place, and yet that couple goes on anyway – broken, damaged, and unsure – but trusting that God may act through and in that decision to love – now that's a *sign from God*. Or when a member of this community suffers a devastating crisis, and this parish rallies to offer prayers, tears, and love – now that's a sign from God Almighty.

Stop asking for a sign –
> and start being one.

In the name of the Father and the Son and the Holy Ghost. *Amen.*

Debris or Decency

Palm Sunday – John J. Capellaro

Let the same mind be in you that was in Christ Jesus …
Philippians 2:5

Let's talk about crowd-mentality and violence. Let's start with the passion of Jesus of Nazareth. Jesus has been traveling and teaching now for just a few years. Some people in Jerusalem know him – but not many. He and his small circle of friends are entering the Holy City this day we call Palm Sunday, headed for what will surely be Jesus' death. Jesus has talked about this inevitability over and over in recent months. He's escaped arrest by the skin of his teeth several times already. Surely this entrance into the city is suicide. So we've got to imagine the emotional level of Jesus' followers is pretty high. They're wound up – full of the Spirit – you might say. Their hero, their friend, their Lord, is entering Jerusalem. He'll either be killed, which is what *he* keeps forecasting – or maybe he'll actually do his Messiah stuff – you know – like maybe restoring the Jews to political superiority after all: an exciting, frightening, and high-pitched time.

In whatever way these things happen, the crowds near the gate to the city begin to catch the energy. Folks gather around Jesus; they become caught up in the mood of the moment; they join in this raucous celebration of the King of the Jews. Jesus' friends allow their own excitement to be cranked up several notches. Maybe they begin to think Jesus doesn't have to die after all. Maybe they begin to forget all that Jesus has been telling them. Before you know it – it's like a parade. Palms are being waved; dozens – maybe even hundreds seem to have caught on to the power of this entrance. Suddenly – almost in an instant, *Jesus' Way* becomes a movement – and it's gaining momentum by the second.

Five days pass. Another large gathering has formed near one of the locations where civil cases are tried and judged. This same man that was being cheered less than a week ago – is now hearing chants from the people of this same city – perhaps even some of the same people: *"Crucify Him! Crucify Him!"*

The remarkable power of crowds! Anyone who has ever attended a football game or political convention knows about the power of crowds. The remarkable power of the common voice! How easily all of us are swept up in the momentum of the voices around us. It may be that the common voice of America is expressed most visibly in our movies and television. It is in these mediums where our true colors are revealed – where we can encounter the most courageous attempt at art and poetry sitting right next to the most thoughtless and crass expressions of pitiable slop and violence our society's most pathetic little minds can create: National Public Radio right next to Howard Stern; *Schindler's List* right next to Adam Sandler's latest dross.

The people of Jerusalem made a choice, when Jesus rode into their Holy City – the City that was meant to represent justice, righteousness, and the very presence of the ever-merciful God. They chose to kill the one who threatened their stability. They chose to join in *the common voice*. It was easier no doubt. It's always more difficult to do the right thing. It's always easier to go along with the crowd. Well, it's our turn. It's our time. And although it's our turn on many different issues, I just want you to make a choice today about one of those issues. And that is what you allow in your homes in the way of published material, videos, music, and television programs. Many parents have adopted the attitude that as our children get older, they will have to make their own decisions about what they'll watch, listen to, or read. Often I've heard good people, people who are perhaps just too busy to die in this particular ditch, say, "Well at least I know they're home if I let them rent this film or listen to that CD." That doesn't cut it. It's lazy and wrong. Left on their own, our children will do what most people do, what most of *us* do, they will become part of the crowd's voice. They will give in. It's just too hard not to.

And this doesn't apply to just those with young people at home. It's just as important for us adults to be discriminating about what we take into our brains and hearts. We know the power of icons, the power of imagery, the power of film, the power of music.   These things have enormous effects on who we are and who we become.   Why would we be anything but discriminating in what we choose to feed ourselves? Something I read this week:

> *A recent survey of more than a thousand studies over a thirty year period has shown decisively that exposure to violent images is associated with anti-social and aggressive behavior.   Movies teach a statistically tiny segment of the population how to kill. [But] the millions of Americans who enjoy screen violence (and I'll add music violence), but are not motivated to imitate it, are NOT unaffected by it.   Like actual violence, screen violence has been shown to anesthetize against empathy with the victim's pain. Moreover, those who watch screen violence and those who perform violent acts have something in common: desensitization.* [1]

Now if you disagree, fine.   If you are one of those who don't believe violence in music or the screen has a negative effect on people, then fine. If you don't believe that petty and diseased talk shows or magazines have a negative effect on people, fine.   In other words, if you know something that contradicts the results of these more than one thousand studies, fine. Write a book.   Enter the dialogue.

But if you do believe that these things have an effect – then do something.   Think about the consequences for a moment.   We wouldn't ingest bits of cancer causing food little by little over a period of years and not expect to contract a disease – would we?   Well for God's sake, why are we doing the same thing with our minds – our hearts – our consciences?   Can you imagine a disease any worse than a desensitized conscience – where empathy and compassion are made even more difficult than they are already?   So if you are persuaded that taking in swill is unhealthy for us – then I ask you to make a decision today.   Make a choice.   It's our turn in history.

Walter Brueggemann, the biblical scholar, writes, "*What God does first and best and most is to trust his people with their moment in history. He trusts them to do what must be done for the sake of his whole*

---

[1] Margaret Miles, *millennium* [3], Volume 2, No.1, Winter 1997.

community."[2]

Well, what are we going to do? I'm asking you to discuss this at home. Make a choice. We can focus on those things that inspire – or we can focus on those things that diminish our humanity. I don't expect the whole society to change – but it's reasonable to expect people of conscience to change. I'm asking you to take responsibility in your own homes and do the right thing – for your children's sake, for your own sake. Do the right thing – for Christ's sake!   *Amen.*

---

[2] Walter Brueggemann, from I'm not sure where! This may be from his book, *Finally Comes the Poet*, or his commentary on *Genesis* for the *Interpretation* series, or perhaps even from my notes that I took during his visit as a guest lecturer in Sewanee. I have looked everywhere and cannot find the source. Sorry, Dr. Brueggemann.

Surely Not I, Lord?

Wednesday in Holy Week – John J. Capellaro

I gave my back to those who struck me, and my cheeks to those who pulled out the beard; I did not hide my face from insult and spitting ... Isaiah 50:6

I wonder if that's a prediction of how the Messiah will act, or a long held value of the Jewish people that reflects how God interacts with us and we are meant to interact with one another. Maybe both. Either way, I don't remember that kind of instruction in my orientations on how to succeed in this world.

> *...he entered once for all into the Holy Place, not with the blood of goats and calves, but with his own blood ... (Hebrews 9:12)*

Now c'mon Jesus, you're never going to inspire followers by being a loser. We're looking for a winner here. You don't get ahead in this life by lying down, let alone by offering yourself up as a sacrifice. It is troubling to see people deliberately posture themselves sacrificially, even when the purpose may be noble. It makes us squirm. We want to send them for assertiveness training. The way to a meaningful life is through clear vision and goals, determination, hard work, and the willingness to fight for what is right. We do not hide our faces from insult and spitting, we ignore them and, more often, spit back.

This journey of faith in YHWH asks for something different. And it is troubling. Selfless behavior – even when it is offered for the sake of others – almost always invites objections and insults, because it threatens all that calls us to safety, stability, and success. I'm reminded of our marriage vows. At the exchange of rings there is a vow the husband and wife offer each other which is:

> *And with all that I am and all that I have I honor you,*
> *in the Name of the Father and the Son, and the Holy Spirit. Amen.*

That's a commitment that upholds the commandment of loving our neighbors as ourselves: to honor the other with all that we are and all that we have, in the Name of God Almighty. Amen. The problem is that selfless behavior of that sort often brings with it insults and spitting. I think of those saints in earlier times, many of them Quakers, who rose up against the tyranny of slavery, and who paid dearly for their commitment to honor the other with all that they had and all that they were.

> *Blessed are those who hunger and thirst for righteousness,*
> *for they will be filled. (Matthew 5:6)*

I think of those people today who are working for an end to capital punishment and who receive insults and spitting, whether standing on the corner of St. Paul's Blvd. and City Hall Avenue, or standing in the halls of government in Richmond.

> *Blessed are the merciful, for they will receive mercy. (Matthew 5:7)*

I think of all those saints who work for justice in our country, striving for a better chance for the homeless, working for changes in our education system – a system that continues to disenfranchise many of our fellow citizens, working for any and all things that allow God's rule to be paramount – and how many of those are on the receiving end of insults and spitting.

> *Blessed are those who are persecuted for righteousness' sake,*
> *for theirs is the kingdom of heaven. (Mathew 5:10)*

I think of those who are coming forward to expose the church for its tyranny – a tyranny that includes sexual abuse, a tyranny that reveals a deep fidelity to worldly power and an apparent disregard for God's, a tyranny that has created a system that uses people's fears and insecurities to inflate itself. And I think of the casual dismissal these people are receiving from their own church. An insult and spit on their faces.

Blessed are you when people revile you and persecute you and utter all kinds of evil against you falsely on my account.

Rejoice and be glad, for your reward is great in heaven, for in the same way they persecuted the prophets who were before you. (Matthew 5:11-12)

To follow Jesus is to join in a movement that opposes many of the values we hold. Security in this life requires power over others, and God's Rule has been revealed in history and in Christ as being opposed to that concept. If we align ourselves with God's ways, we will be spit upon, for it threatens the ways of the world. And none of us are exempt.

Every time we laugh at a joke about people who are different than us, we are doing the spitting. Eevery time we complain about church needing to be a place of solace alone and not a tempest of protest against injustice, we are doing the spitting. Every time we accept the poverty which surrounds us as a natural part of life, we are doing the spitting. Every time we run from the chance to get our hands dirty in the ugly and risky business of following God in Christ, we are doing the spitting.

And Jesus said to his disciples, "Truly I tell you, one of you will betray me."

And they became greatly distressed and began to say to him one after another, "Surely not I, Lord?" (Matthew 26:21-22)

And so with Judas today, we come to you Lord and ask, "Are we betraying you – again? Are we the ones doing the spitting? Is it I, Lord? Is it I?"

Grit and Grime

Maundy Thursday – Patricia R. Davis

He came to Simon Peter, who said to him, "Lord, are you going to wash my feet?" Jesus answered, "You do not know now what I am doing, but later you will understand." John 13:6

One of the perks of membership at St. Paul's is a parking place for MacArthur Mall. And right across the street is a store with a shoe department to inspire hope in any man or woman. Now shoe stores are one of my favorite places. Personally, I have 6 pairs of black shoes and I'm still looking for a pair that will be comfortable all day long! And it's fascinating to me that we spend so much time and money trying to dress up and cover up a most utilitarian part of ourselves. Now it's not often that you hear a sermon about body parts but tonight I'm going to talk, as you may have guessed, about feet.

This rite of foot washing is one of the least attended, least liked rituals of our church. Getting people to come forward and have their feet washed is like asking people to voluntarily undergo a root canal ... we don't get many takers! And it seems that even the disciples had some reservations about this common custom being acted out by their rabbi. After all, this was a custom that was a measure of hospitality and they had all forgotten to do it in their distraction and self-absorption. Luke tells us that on the way they were caught up in arguing about who was the best of the disciples, who would be the greatest in relationship to Jesus.

We've all known meals like this. We bring some unsettled argument or deeply wounded feelings to the dinner table and it's nothing like the family meal we know it should be. This foot washing was not a last kindness done by Jesus in the warm company of those who loved and supported him and would see him through. This was a strained dinner table at which conversation comes haltingly and sparingly and hearts are breaking all over the place. They had invested their lives following this man who promised a better world and here he was talking about an end they couldn't imagine, a grim and futile betrayal of all their hopes. It's natural to turn inward, to wrap up in cloaks of self-protection and just try to get through it all without getting hurt anymore. And then, Jesus, in the middle of this silent and sorrowful meal, got up. According to some translations, he took off, not just his outer robe, but his clothes. He wrapped a towel around his exposed and vulnerable body and knelt at their feet and began to wash them.

Jesus silently came around with a basin of water and they reacted as we do tonight, with stunned, flinching participation – except for Peter, who at least had the decency to feel guilty. And Jesus washed all their dirty, world-stained feet and then he asked them, "Do you know what I have done?" And the answer to that question is worthy of lots and lots of sermons but I want to suggest one thing that Jesus did when he washed their feet. What Jesus did, I think, was to confront his people's hidden, painfully human lives.

But back to the feet. Now it seems to me that when my feet hurt, my whole body hurts! And I think that's metaphorically true too. Our feet are the world-weary symbol of all of ourselves. Our feet tell the tale of our work and our pain and often it's not a pretty picture. But we keep trying to make our feet, and our lives, look better than they really are. Like a ballerina's feet. Have you ever seen a ballerina's feet? Underneath those beautiful pink satin toe shoes are calluses, ingrown nails and blisters that bleed as she dances. But you don't have to be a ballerina to do this. We all do this. We cover up our feet with fancy footwear or, in summer sandal weather, try to pretty up our feet if they must be bared. In the same way, we try to cover up or pretty up our raw or callused inside places.

But when the feet hurt, the whole body is in pain. And we're taught from day one to keep our pain and dirt hidden. We hide it from our neighbors. Some of us have gotten pretty good at hiding it from ourselves, and in our stranger moments, we even think we can keep it hidden from God. It's as though we want to show God only the cleaned up, dressed up version of ourselves and when he suggests that he might need to tend to all of us, we flinch and say, "Never, Lord!"

We don't want anyone to see our dirty feet. Our dirty feet are the things we'd rather not look at, if the truth be known. Our dirty feet can take the form of yelling at a loved one or snapping at a friend or co-worker. Our dirty feet can look like despair over our child or hopelessness at the state of the world. Our dirty feet can look like resentment at yet another plea for help from the church or like refusal to work on a committee with that person! Our dirty feet are all the things about ourselves we'd just as soon keep hidden, even from ourselves. We carry around a lot of grime in our shoes and Jesus comes along with a basin of warm water and offers to wash it all off and we look away.

If there is anything we need to know about this lesson, it's this: living with God is about meeting life's dirtiness up close and personal. And it's so awfully hard to do. Just consider: this wafer and this cup that we so reverently consume are really an earthy loaf and a homemade wine, and underneath that is a bleeding, wounded savior. And this disciple business is all about dirty feet and souls in pain, with a lot of other brothers and sisters we'd rather not be around if we can help it. But notice that Jesus washed the feet of Judas, too. There is no one who's so dirty that he's excluded from God's tending, unless he excludes himself. God approaches each of us, over and over again, basin in hand, offering to wash our feet. It's that kind of family too, one that persists in self-giving love in the face of the world's evil.

So Jesus breaks in on our strained family supper, not a wimpy, sweet sort of savior but a gritty companion, a fellow sufferer, a man whose feet will soon bear the scars of all our pain. He's been here all the time, see, and he wants us to show him our dirty feet. To let Him wash them. He comes toward us with a basin of water and his body bared and he says, "You must let me do this for you. It's the only way you can be part of me." And everything in us says, "Run the other way!"

But He keeps coming. He asks us again to let him look at our dirty feet, to look at them ourselves if we can bear it, and see what he sees: wounded souls worth dying for. As we sit in the uncomfortable silent spaces we leave in our worship service, I ask one thing: let it be a time when we dare to let Jesus come near. He is coming, basin in hand, and he only asks that we take off our shoes and show him our dirty feet. *Amen.*

The Power of Weakness

Good Friday – John J. Capellaro

He was oppressed, and he was afflicted, yet he did not open his mouth; like a lamb that is led to the slaughter, and like a sheep that before its shearers is silent, so he did not open his mouth. Isaiah 53:7

One of the tourist sites in Jerusalem is a very small room with a tile floor that has carvings in the floor. Our tour guide described it as a "Game Room." It seems that when prisoners were awaiting execution, they would be taken to one of these "Game Rooms," where soldiers made a game of torturing the prisoners. The task of killing had become so routine that they'd invented a game of torture to play with the prisoners in the hours preceding their death. The carvings in the tile floor revealed the pattern of rules, much like a board game might today. As each player won points, he was awarded permission to inflict some bit of torture on the prisoner.

Jesus was held in one of these Game Rooms before his execution. It was there where he was likely beaten, whipped, spit upon, and whatever else the imaginations of those soldiers may have produced – and whatever our imaginations may permit. This was all done with the knowledge and at least the implicit permission of the Roman leadership and even the Temple officials. This practice of making a game of torture had become "normal."

Funny how such things can become "normal." It seems that anything can become acceptable given the right circumstances. I suppose it's how slavery survived here in America, with so many accepting it as "normal." Conscience is easily duped. Trifles such as "Custom" and "Tradition," often become the food and nourishment for fear, hatred, and aberrant behavior. Do we think this phenomenon was limited to the Romans, or can be found only among radical religious fundamentalists today? Do we not all have blind spots, masked in custom or tradition that continue to eat away at conscience?

> *All we like sheep have gone astray;*
> *we have all turned to our own way.* (Isaiah 53:6)

Do we not all participate in games that pretend to award superiority, power, security, and being right – over against those who are wrong? The community of John, whose gospel we read today, insists that Jesus is the unique agent of God, and that his place among us gives us an example of God among us. And so how does he behave? What is the example of how to live that we are offered by God's unique agent? Weakness. Jesus bears the worst of humanity through weakness. He receives – takes on – all that feeds hate and fear, and lets it be exposed as futile. God's agent yields to the fears of reform within his own religious community. He yields to the power of the state. He yields to our games. That's God's example. Power over others is always fleeting; power over others always becomes corrupted. Benevolent power is an oxymoron. Beneficence is possible only in servitude. Power is possible only in weakness. Love survives. Nothing else.

The Love of God, which we see in Jesus, is undiminished by the desertion of his apostles, the rejection of his beloved people, or the mockery of those who make a game of torturing him. God's perfection is in weakness. God is vulnerable. The games we play, aimed at establishing or celebrating superiority are vulgar – and ultimately in vain. To digest this message intellectually is a lifetime's work. To live this way – to live this way … Can you imagine? To follow Christ – to sit at the Cross and come face to face with how backwards we actually live – to recognize it and then do more than simply say, "Ah well, but what other way is there?"

Today we acknowledge that our relationship with God hinges on death – and not just the death of Jesus – but our death. It hinges on looking at all that defines us – family name, personal reputation, Church – all of it, and then seeing how much of what supports and nourishes these ideas, values, and mythologies of ours are rooted in notions of superiority, power and strength. The example we have in the god-man says, "All of it is useless, folks." The game of finding security in those temporal things is futile; the game of self-promotion is, by definition, commingled with fear and hatred. Our hope is in weakness. The strategy that God reveals to us, facing our weakness, seeking and then bringing it to God, to the Cross, bringing all our broken promises, and our dashed hopes, our violence and anger, and our deepest fears, all the shameful games in which we are sometimes victim, and often player. Only then do we begin our walk with Christ. In facing, perhaps even embracing, those weaknesses, we begin to live as if God is God and we aren't. This Good Friday liturgy invites us to be carried away to the presence of God in Christ – on the Cross. To be reconciled to God through weakness and death.

Ecce Homo – Here is the Man, Pilate tells us. Look at him. May we offer him our games. May we taste God's victory in Christ's weakness and then in our own. May we be *God's* children once more. *Amen.*

Still Standing

Good Friday – Patricia R. Davis

...standing near the cross of Jesus were his mother, and his mother's sister, Mary the wife of Clopas, and Mary Magdalene ... and the disciple whom he loved standing beside [his mother]. John 19:25

"Were you there when they crucified my Lord?" Well, of course, we weren't there. We have a partial list of those who were there. It includes a lot of women, the usual gawkers at any public execution, the soldiers and people in charge of making sure that everything went smoothly, with a minimum of trouble, but not us. We weren't there and most of us say, "Thank God, I didn't have to see that." And underneath it all, maybe "Thank God, I didn't have to make that choice." Because it was an awful choice to be there. Two thousand years later, it's all we can do to come to a beautiful building and sit in comfort and listen to the terrible story. It's a day most of us would just as soon skip, and many do, preferring to go from the triumphal entry as a king into Jerusalem to the joyous proclamation of Easter day, ignoring the massive shadow of the cross that falls on everything in between. "Were you there when they crucified my Lord?" Thank God we weren't there.

Perhaps it's a bit demented of me, but I've always wondered how I would have reacted. I've always wondered if I would have had the courage to stand at the foot of the cross, to watch my dreams die, and still to place my life in his hands. Would I be strong enough? Would I have what it takes to risk everything for the sake of someone who is leaving me? How far does my trust in God's saving grace go? Is my faith founded on anything more than some warm fuzzy Christmas feelings and some great Easter songs? Sometimes I'm much more "Doubting Thomas" than

94

faithful disciple.

But 3 years ago, my best friend died of cancer. And I realized as I stood at the foot of her hospital bed, that I was watching a crucifixion. Since then I've come to see that there are a lot of people who stand at the foot of the cross. And they are ordinary people whose faithfulness comes one painful, halting step at a time, one long, exhausting day at a time. They are people who go to the foot of the cross because there is no place else they can be.

Where is the foot of the cross? It can be in the nursing home where there is a young woman, about 40 now, whose mother visits every day. Her daughter has MS and can no longer eat or drink, talk or swallow; she has even lost the ability to smile. Her husband couldn't cope. Shortly after she was diagnosed, he divorced her. Who can blame him? He didn't sign on for a lifetime of celibacy, visiting his wife in a nursing home and caring for their girls alone. But her mother is there every day, standing at the foot of the cross.

Many in our own parish and in our own neighborhoods are standing at the foot of the cross. There are spouses who awake every day to a round of care-taking chores that would break the backs of any of us, because their mates are disabled. There is the foot of the cross. There are grandmothers who care for grandchildren while their own children break their hearts. There is the foot of the cross. There are people whose loved ones suffer with Alzheimer's disease or simply the ravages of time. There are people fighting abuse and neglect in a hundred different disguises. They are all standing at the foot of the cross. There are no soaring symphonies playing in the background of these scenes, only deadly weariness and tears that just won't stop. They are all standing at the foot of the cross. The foot of the cross is that place where we risk having our hearts broken in two because the one suffering is part of that very heart. The foot of the cross is that place where we declare ourselves willing to keep company with agony, in His name. And because, like the first disciples, there is no imagining anything after this grief but more grief, the sky is dark and the curtain of caring hearts torn in two.

These are occasions of immense courage. To stare into the heart of hopelessness and still stand. To look into the depths of despair and fall on our knees, crushed but still there. To bear witness to life's grimmest realities, simply because bearing witness is what *must* be done ... this is courage with a godly strength.

It is a courage born of knowing the man called Jesus and trusting, when trust seems the stupidest thing to do, that God is in this somewhere. It is knowing that by his wounds we are healed, though the healing is unto death. It is hoping, when Easter is still an unimaginable possibility. Because there is no place else to be in times like these but standing at the foot of the cross.

After today, we will move gratefully (we would hurry it if we could) away from this gruesome story and into Easter joy. But there are those who must still stand at the foot of the cross. Let us acknowledge their courage, their faithfulness, with our own lives. Please God, let us go to them, and choose to stand with them, hold them up in their grief by bearing witness that the worst that life has to offer is not beyond the love of God.

Christ has died and though it makes no sense at all, because he died we can live ... today at the foot of the cross ... tomorrow in darkest grief. We live by looking to a bloody hill and a borrowed tomb, from whence our help comes.   *Amen*

EASTER

What Is the Meaning of This?!?!

Easter Day – John J. Capellaro

Alleluia! Christ is Risen.
The Lord is risen indeed. Alleluia!

What meaning does that acclamation hold for you?

An old friend of mine called me recently from his hotel room in New York. He'd just moved into his Park Avenue suite, having left his wife and two children. It was a *very* fine hotel. My friend is accustomed to the better things in life. He's a graduate of an Ivy League school. The home he and his wife shared for many years is in one of those "important" neighborhoods in the New York City suburbs. They've sent both their children to the very best academies – the one's where you have to know someone to get on the waiting list, and you have to register your children *for* that waiting list at the moment of conception. You know the type?

I was surprised by his call, not only because we hadn't spoken in about five years, but also by what he had to tell me. He talked about why he was leaving his family. He offered his rationale with a confident tone, as if he'd just solved a complex puzzle. "Well John," he offered thoughtfully, "You know, I have a house in the suburbs, nice cars, a wife, two kids. We have a healthy portfolio, take great vacations – but it just seems like there should be something else. This can't be all there is … So I've decided to explore some other options." When I asked him what his plans were, he said, "I think I'll try life in the city for a while. So I'm going to keep my home base here at the hotel for the next few months. But I'm also going to Paris for a few weeks, just to clear my head. I've always liked Paris."

As I listened to his yearning for meaning in his life, my heart broke.

99

I wanted to scream, "*Alleluia. Christ has risen,*" but then I realized he didn't have that vocabulary. That acclamation wouldn't hold much meaning for him.

We've all anguished over the meaning in our lives at one time or another, and some of us are in a chronic state of anguish over the quest for meaning. And we can all share stories about where we've found meaning. I suspect that most of us would say that our families, and the relationships with spouses, parents or children, in some way hold the most meaning for us. That's certainly true for me. Many would probably comment on their careers. I've heard some powerful stories about the meaning many people derive from their work. As someone who has changed careers specifically in search of more meaning, I certainly understand that one. But is there more than family, career, goals for a healthy retirement, or hopes of grandchildren? What difference does it make that "*Christ has risen?*" Does it make you want to say, "*Alleluia?*" Or is it an assurance of life after death – so we can come to church whenever we can fit it into our schedules and check it off as yet one more thing we've taken care of – as if it's just a feature of good "post-retirement" planning. Do church and our Christian story offer any meaning?

Following the 11th of September, churches, mosques, temples, and synagogues were filled. And a few weeks later – once folks had a chance to mourn – or give church one more try – or whatever it was that brought them there, things went back to "normal." It seems that church has failed to inspire, or maybe there's just more meaning to be found in shopping, buying the new SUV, or planning that trip – maybe even to Paris. *Alleluia. Christ has risen.*

I don't know what's brought you all here today. Some of you may be looking for meaning; others may have all the meaning you can handle at the moment. Some may have been dragged here against your will. And a few may have just needed a place to wear that new outfit. God knows, I understand that source of meaning! Whatever your reasons, I just want to offer a few examples of the meaning that some folks I know are discovering here in churchland, because it continues to surprise me.

There are people in this community who continue to be outraged at political oppression and the fact of hunger in the world. They are unsettled by the fact that over the past six years, 25,000 people have died from acts of political and religious terrorism.   They are even more unsettled that over that same period, more than 24,000,000 people starved to death.   This group organized themselves into a team that sponsored four young men from the Sudan, who had been living in a refugee camp in Kenya for the past ten years, to move here to Norfolk. This team has worked many hours, sacrificed a number of personal plans, and has made an extraordinary difference in the lives of these four men – and in the life of this faith community.   Bagfuls of meaning have emerged from their commitment. *Alleluia.   Christ is risen?*

There are people in this community who come together week in and week out to study.   These men and women don't take literally what they hear in Scripture, nor do they approach it as irrelevant ancient writings. Out of their regard for scholarship, they have come to discover a significant value in these writings – and in one another.   They are developing skills to face the bigger questions in life with a new maturity that embraces the value of history, traditions, and diverse friendships, and many of them are surprised by what they are learning. *Alleluia. Christ is risen.*

There's a person in what he called a "difficult" marriage.   He was pretty sure he'd just married the wrong woman. After a couple of years of prayer – "sacred listening" as some call it – he is coming to believe that a good marriage doesn't depend so much on finding the right partner as it does on being one.   I can tell you that isn't the answer he came to church looking for.   His discovery is changing the way he approaches a number of things in his life. *Alleluia! Christ has risen.*

A woman from my former parish in Pennsylvania longed for a child so deeply that it consumed her marriage.   She couldn't be a full person without being a mother. After several failed pregnancies and three years of reflection, and interaction with other mothers she came to the insight that her wholeness did not depend on being a parent – but rather being a parent depended on her wholeness.   Shortly after that spiritual discovery she became pregnant.   She and her husband now have two children – one adopted – the second one – and they are both learning how to become parents. *Alleluia! Christ is risen.*

There are a number of people in *this* community who are living with serious illness and who have discovered extraordinary meaning, sometimes even physical benefits, in this community's holding them in prayer. *Alleluia! Christ is risen!*

There are people in this community who, a little over a year ago, were asked if they might want to work with our new youth group SPY (*Saint Paul's Youth*). They didn't know exactly what was in store – but then again neither did we. This June, six adults and 18 teenagers are traveling to Utah to work for 12 days in a Navajo work camp. All the volunteers are giving up their vacation to do this, and many have made contributions towards the cost of this trip. What would drive these young men and women to spend their summer vacation this way? Have they seen God interacting with our teenagers? Has God touched them? What is the meaning of their offering? I'll let you ask them. *Alleluia! Christ is risen!*

Many of us, who avoided church for a while have discovered great richness in our story and sacraments, richness we may have missed as children. We've discovered people of great intellect and remarkable heart in "churchland," who have found meaning in their faith communities to live in ways that have nourished them and those around them – people who are making a difference in the world. We've seen that regular engagement with our sacred stories and sacraments changes us. We've met people for whom "new life" is neither fluff nor fairy tale – people who have opened their minds and hearts to the possibility of God's real presence in the world. I realize that the meaning offered to us in church may not offer the instant gratification of a new SUV; the meaning found in church may not be as physically stimulating an extramarital affair or a round of golf, or as emotionally satisfying as watching the kids at a Sunday morning soccer game; the meaning available in a committed relationship with church is certainly not as fashionable as a few weeks in Paris ... but it does offer an arena in which the bigger questions in life are at the center of our dialogue. It offers the stories that have shaped people for thousands of years, and it offers the rites that recall, relive, and allow those stories to breathe with our breath – with *your* breath ...

God is present and available. There is hope. I believe that God cares deeply about how we spend our time and whether or not we discover the meaning that is intended for our lives. The Easter story is waiting to take root in each one of us. Jesus the Christ has been rejected and killed. And God's judgment for his people is mercy.

Love survives.

New life abounds.

Meaning awaits us all.

Alleluia! Christ is risen. The Lord is risen indeed. Alleluia!
Alleluia! Christ is risen. The Lord is risen indeed. Alleluia!
Alleluia! Christ is risen. The Lord is risen indeed. Alleluia!

God, With Skin On

Season of Easter – Patricia R. Davis

So the other disciples told him, "We have seen the Lord." But he said to them, "Unless I see the mark of the nails in his hands, and put my finger in the mark of the nails and my hand in his side, I will not believe." John 20:25

When I was in high school, I decided to change my name. I was tired of being *Patti*. I wanted to be *Tricia*. I knew other girls named *Tricia* and they were everything I wasn't. *Patti* was short, "cute," unsophisticated and definitely uncool. *Tricia* was classy, sophisticated, mysterious and definitely cool. But somehow, it never caught on. So I have a lot of sympathy for Thomas, who was known as "the Twin" but who could have been known as "Devoted Thomas." Because this is the same Thomas who, of all the disciples, declared himself ready to go with Jesus to Jerusalem and die with him. But when we meet him in this story fully 2000 years later, he wears a nametag that reads "Doubting Thomas." I hope he will forgive us for sticking him with a name that belongs in fact to all the disciples, and that belongs, quite often, to us.

When the gospel story opens, all of the disciples except Thomas are gathered behind closed doors. They aren't acting like people who heard the good news of the resurrection from the women at the tomb. They're acting like frightened, disbelieving people. The scripture says, "…the doors of the house where the disciples had met were locked [in] fear…" Then Jesus comes and shows them his wounds and finally they believe what they have already been told. But Thomas wasn't there and when he hears this incredible story, he doesn't believe them. He could be any

104

one of us. He's seen the results of crucifixion and he knows that it meant the death of Jesus' body and the death of his own soul. Resurrection was beyond the bounds of belief, without some proof other than the ranting of a group of desperate, grieving friends who were probably ashamed of their own betrayal of Jesus. So he says those famous words, "Unless I see the mark of the nails in his hands, and put my finger in the mark of the nails and my hand in his side, I will not believe."

It all reminds me of one of my favorite stories, about a little boy who was prone to nightmares. One night he woke up yet again, crying because of some fearful thing he had dreamed, and his mother came in to comfort him. *Please, Mommy*, he asked, *can I come and sleep in the big bed with you?* *Honey*, she said, *you know you don't ever have to be afraid, no matter where you are. Because wherever you are, Jesus is there with you. I know*, he said, *but right now I need some skin on him!*

This little boy was saying what Thomas was honest enough to say and what we all wish for at times: *Please God, put some skin on so I can know for sure that you're real.* We need something identifiable, some wounds on the hands, some scar on his side, some sign, something that will reassure us. If we are to follow him, like Thomas, to Jerusalem and beyond, we need to know at least once in a while that this story that we tell over and over, year after year, has some truth to it that we can hang on to. And the story is beautiful and inspiring. Who can fail to be moved by shepherds watching in the fields by night, a sweet baby born to a young, trusting mother, sick people healed, a parade with people waving and singing, a quiet meal together with those he loved. They are powerful stories. But then we come here on the Sunday morning after Easter and our husband has just lost his job or our father is still sick and hurting or our child has brought us to the precipitous edge of our sanity and we have to stand up and say "We believe …" – and it's hard to do. Here we are, declaring ourselves confident in a god we can't see, whose wounds we've only heard about but never touched. Every once in a while, for God's sake, we need some skin on him!

So … this is how far I had gotten on this sermon when I went in to work on Thursday. And, as I often do, I asked God to please show me why it was that I was there that day. *Please, Lord, give me a clue about what it is I'm doing here.* And so I spent the day listening to people cry.

And when I asked them where God was in all of this, this is what I heard: I heard them say that God wasn't happy with them because

      a) they didn't have enough faith,

      b) they had done some terrible things in their lives and

      c) God would forgive them only if they quit making mistakes.

And when I said how lonely that all sounded, I heard: *God, how I wish someone would just hug me!*

Merciful heavens! What were they saying but the same thing that the disciples were feeling and that Thomas was brave enough to verbalize; namely, that we have sorely failed at believing God and we need some skin on him to know he's still here with us!

So we take ourselves back to this story, back to the locked room that suddenly became filled with the presence of Christ and now we find the answers to the dilemma of belief and doubt. Because we see Jesus looking at us too, as he holds out his hands to Thomas and we hear him say, *Peace be with you.* Remember that? Before everything else, before dealing with the doubt and fear, before dealing with our shame at falling short, before anything else, Jesus says *Peace*; in other words, *Rest easy, I still love you.* How hard that is to believe! We can believe that God would condemn us for our doubt more easily than we can believe that he loves us. God, who gives us Christmas and Easter and walks with us every step of the road in between, loves us!

So I want you to hear this about belief. Belief isn't about agreeing with a set of esoteric ideas about God, but about our hearts. To believe is simply to give our hearts to the source of all our yearning, whether we understand that source or not.

It's when we know that, when we give him our heart, that we discover that God has had his skin on all the time. We discover that he's been waiting for us in the hug of a friend and the smile of a stranger. We find that he reaches out his wounded hands as a companion in our grief or simply a companion through a hard day. We learn that he values our questions much more than our good behavior, and that he will never leave us.

And surprisingly enough, he even puts on our skin from time to time. We look down and discover that the things that have wounded our hearts have also left the mark of His redemptive love on us. That what makes us cry and what makes us afraid and what makes us doubt are the doors through which Jesus comes once again.   That we also wear a nametag, by virtue of our baptism, by virtue of who we have given our heart to, and that name tag is forever engraved on our foreheads: *Christ's Own*. We are marked as Christ's own forever.

And with God's blessing and the grace of his vision, we may even come to see that we can bring the presence of Christ into all kinds of strange and unimaginable places, because we come to understand that Jesus may use us, may use our skin to walk around in.   He may use us to hug someone lonely, to feed someone hungry in body and spirit, to wipe the tears of someone so very tired.

Thomas, bless his heart, is our stand-in, the man who said what we were afraid to think. And through Thomas, we learn God's answer to our doubt: we discover that we're not locked away alone but in the company of other disciples who have tried and failed and still, the Lord has graciously come among us.   We can leave that locked room, with companions for the journey and with a mission and a message.   Christ has died, Christ is risen, Christ is coming into the world.   *Amen*

Conversion? No, Thank You. I'm Fine

Season of Easter – John J. Capellaro

… Ananias laid his hands on Saul and said, "Brother Saul, the Lord Jesus, who appeared to you on your way here, has sent me so that you may regain your sight and be filled with the Holy Spirit." And immediately something like scales fell from his eyes, and his sight was restored. Then he got up and was baptized, and after taking some food, he regained his strength.
Acts 9:17-19a

He took everything too seriously. He was one of those men who wouldn't be satisfied until he discovered meaning for his life. You know the type? He held fervent beliefs about everything; people described him as "intense." You couldn't be around this guy for more than five minutes without him bringing up something that would raise an eyebrow. He insisted that you face the hard questions in life, whether you wanted to or not. You just wanted to say to him, "Lighten up; take a chill pill." The really sad thing was that he didn't have to be this way. He was well educated and his family knew lots of people in positions of influence. Although he wasn't much to look at, even as a young man, he was very bright and had a number of opportunities to fit into the main stream, if he had just played the game. But he insisted on being a royal pain. You know the type? Then worst of all, he became fervent about religion. You know what happens when people become a little too fervent about religion. At some point, there's going to be trouble, and sure enough, "Mr. Intense" was no exception. It seems that some people were beginning to get some new ideas about this man's religion that made him very uncomfortable. So our friend set himself to straightening them out. But being the intense guy he was, he went to extremes. He actually came into towns where he was a stranger and persuaded the local authorities to give him names of those who were suspected of having these new ideas. Then he'd go to their homes, have them bound and gagged and taken into custody. These people were then tried, and if convicted, dismissed from their faith communities, which, for most, meant they lost their incomes, since their businesses depended on other church members. There were some instances where the people this man accused were actually killed in the streets, like rabid dogs. This man became hated and feared by many – and we have named our church for him. But not because of the behavior I have just described, of course. This man, Saul, had an experience of conversion that brought all he held sacred to its knees. Driven by one set of values, Saul is suddenly faced with the recognition that all he has held to be true and accurate, all that he was certain about, is revealed as misguided and wrong. Saul, the enemy of Jesus Christ, becomes Paul, the instrument of Christ's mission.

Sometimes conversion turns us 180 degrees from where we were, and leaves us gifted with new sight to see how blind we've been. The power of God is real – and present. God will overcome the certainty of Saul – as well as my certainty and yours. Zealots will not inhibit God's Reign. Nations cannot contain God's Sovereignty. God's Rule will not be managed – even by religions. God's people will be converted. And if you think that things are fine, and you hope that God isn't looking to work any conversion in you; if you've got enough people stirring the pot in your life right now; if the reason you come to church is to be reminded that you are loved and that things are really okay, well, you're in good company. We all need that. But I don't think we can get away with only being reminded that God loves us no matter what. There is a need for conversion in the world – in America – in you and me. A few fun thoughts from a book entitled, *The Call to Conversion*, published eight years ago:

> *The same [American] companies that make things to delight the rich also make things to defend them. Texas Instruments, a producer of electronic games, also makes guided missile systems aimed at other people's children. General Electric ("We bring Good Things to Life") manufactures not only ... early morning*

coffeemakers but also the Mark 12-A missile, a first strike nuclear weapon.

The author of this book suggests:

The logic is clear. Our [American] affluence must be protected if we are to control the lion's share of the world's resources and leave a billion people hungry. We cannot create an economy based on over consumption without creating the weapons necessary to keep the poor masses at bay ... Behind our cheery TV commercials lies a quiet, deadly reality.[1]

Is the freedom for which so many have died – a freedom to be more affluent – at the expense of others? When we say our national security is threatened, what is it exactly that's threatened most? Are not the values espoused in our life of abundance formative for our children? Has not our American way of life become more about security, comfort, and product, than it has about benevolence, justice, sacrifice, and spiritual growth?

Who of us is not in need of conversion?

It sometimes feels like modern American Christianity has become a well-orchestrated conspiracy to smother conversion. It's okay to have a conversion experience – providing you don't begin to live differently. Most fervent Christians, people we would assume know something about conversion, seem to have made Christianity into a vehicle for getting into heaven – rather than a movement meant to reveal God's Kingdom here and now. For much of Christianity, Jesus is the agent for salvation rather than the agent for God's Reign. Remember that the biblical references to the Kingdom of God or the Kingdom of Heaven refer to that existence where God is in charge – and that existence begins here and now. God's Rule is the consequence of conversion – now. Focusing our religion on the afterlife seems a good way to avoid the challenges which result from conversion to Jesus' way of life. It's not that the next life isn't

---

[1] Jim Wallis, *The Call to Conversion* (San Francisco: HarperSanFrancisco, 1992), xiii.

important. It's just out of our hands. There's nothing we can do or not do to influence God's Grace. We may be able to develop disciplines that allow us to experience God's Grace more fully – disciplines like prayer – regular participation in communion – making a confession, but we cannot manage or manipulate God's Grace. It's God's gift. Period.

I suppose that if conversion is to be embraced as the beginning of a faith journey, we'll have to decide if our Christianity is going to have anything to do with Jesus; if so, then our Christian faith must address present realities, because after all, Jesus is God breaking into history – here and now. The church continues to lose credibility with many because of our history of dismissing issues of social justice as non-religious. Education for the poor, economic justice, capital punishment, racism ... these are religious issues – at least they are for Christians. The degree to which we pretend they are not, is the degree to which we distance ourselves from Jesus and God's Kingdom.[2] Conversion to Jesus leads us to love one another, and loving one another necessarily eats away at the social status quo. I believe God calls us all to conversion, and I think our resistance to conversion runs deep. We are practiced at denying God's calls in our lives, and I think the church helps us with that denial. I think that many of the people who *are* listening to God's call have their conversion neutered by a church that has more incentive to maintain the status quo than not. The good news is that God's Reign will not be neutered; God's Kingdom will not be contained, managed, distributed, or diluted – even by church. God will continue to convert Samaritans and zealots like Saul. God will find Ethiopian eunuchs, and people will be drawn to God's reign, because it brings with it light and life. I suppose *our* challenge is to find the courage and trust to accept the changes that conversion to Jesus demands.

As John Henry Newman offered, "To live is to change ... and to be perfect is to have changed often." The power of God is real – and present. Nothing will inhibit God's Reign. Nations cannot contain God's Sovereignty. God's Rule will not be managed – even by Christianity. God overcomes the certainty of Saul – as well as my certainty and yours.

We will be converted. *Amen.*

---

[2] Paraphrase of another passage from *The Call to Conversion*. See pages xiv-xv.

Strife Closed in the Sod

Season of Easter – Patricia R. Davis

Peace I leave with you; my peace I give to you. I do not give to you as the world gives. John 14:27

Many of you have known me for 2 years or more now, but there's much you don't know. I'm a wife and mother and Deacon, yes, but I'm also the oldest daughter of Genevieve and Walter Rhoads. From my mother I get my artistic talents, my love of beauty and my sense of humor. From my father I have inherited my looks, my drive to do things well and my introverted nature. My grandparents were of German, Norwegian, Swiss and English extraction– from them I received my name, my light hair, my work ethic and my small stature, to name a few characteristics. I had a great-grandfather who was a Baptist minister of some renown in Pennsylvania, so maybe some of that spiritual yearning of mine can be traced a long way back. All of these ancestors of mine eventually made a home in this country, raised their families and tried to pass on the things that they deemed important. When I began to think about what I had inherited, I also began to think about what I was passing on. I asked my oldest daughter, Genevieve, to help me with this and the list is not quite so impressive as I might have hoped! It turns out that I have passed on my klutziness, and what many would deem an odd way of looking at the world! I've passed on my obsessive-compulsive tendencies – which I prefer to call "organizational skills." I've also passed on some artistic talent, a love of reading and, I hope, a wealth of good memories. Such is some of my children's inheritance from me.

What we're hearing here, in the reading from the Gospel of John, is Jesus, passing out his inheritance. He is soon to lose what little he has.

Even his clothes will be divided up among people who aren't his family, yet he still has something to pass on. *Peace*, he says, *Peace I leave with you; my peace I give to you.* Our inheritance from Jesus.

So what does Jesus mean by peace? He certainly didn't have a peaceful life or, that hope of all of us, a peaceful death. His life was filled with incredible demands from all quarters: with requests for healing, questions from friends who didn't understand what he was about, constant challenges to his view of the world. He never had a home he could retreat to, a place where his favorite possessions made him feel secure – he found himself staying with whoever offered a bed for the night, often with some unsavory characters. He hadn't any money to speak of but depended on the charity of others. He had few clothes and even those were taken from him, to be replaced by a hat of thorns and a coat of mockery. Even his dearest friends abandoned him at the end, running away in fear. This we can better understand. We know insecurity and we've felt fear. They're much more common than any kind of peace.

Like people everywhere, then and now, we have too many demands on our time, energy and attention. We have homes, yes, but they more often seem to need more work rather than being places of refuge. We have possessions that possess us, frequent worry over whether we will be able to afford all that life seems to demand, the recurring feeling that we must go more, do more, be more in order to be OK. Peace is a commodity in short supply for most of us and I suspect that most of us can't imagine the peace Jesus was talking about, much less make room for it. Yet peace is what Jesus talked about in a way that you knew it was his to give. This was his final bequest. Peace is what Jesus wants us to inherit and to pass on from him. Peace is what we dare to offer each other in the middle of the service!

So what is this peace and what would it look like? We have some clues in the lessons today. It is not "as the world gives." In other words, all of our chasing after security, all of our *everything will be fine if only...* these are not an answer. God's peace is not found in those elements of life that we have come to think of as denoting success. Physical and fiscal success may make us more comfortable, but they are no guarantee of peace. This peace is "not as the world gives."

Neither is this peace a simple optimism, a Pollyanna looking-for-the-silver-lining kind of approach. This is a tough, gritty, grappling-with-evil kind of peace. This is the peace that prompted Julian Of Norwich, living in a time of poverty and plague, to say *All will be well. And all will be well. And all manner of thing will be well.* It's the sort of peace that moved Mother Teresa to walk the streets of the dying in Calcutta and that moves the nurses where I work to walk the halls, in spite of low pay and killing hours. It's the kind of peace that stirs someone confined to a single bed in a single room to take on the world in prayer, every day. It's the sort of peace that enables spouses and parents to keep on loving when loving seems all too hard. All of these have accepted their inheritance, have owned up to being children of God. They have come to learn what it is to be gifted with that "peace that passes understanding." It's a peace that remains confident in God's redeeming work, though everything in the world would testify otherwise.

St. Paul described this peace in his letter to the Corinthians:

> harassed on all sides, but not crushed;
> plunged in doubt, but not despairing;
> persecuted, but not forsaken;
> struck down, but not destroyed;
> as dying, but see, we live;
> as punished, but not put to death;
> as poor, yet making many rich;
> as having nothing and yet possessing everything.

As you may have gathered by now, this isn't peace by any of our conventional definitions. It takes some courage to accept this inheritance from Jesus. This peace that he wants to give us is not freedom from trouble or worry; in fact, it may be found right alongside trouble.

But it is peace. It's a disturbing kind of peace. It often accompanies a call to a deeper relationship with the Lord. And God may take us where we think we don't want to go, like into a nursing home or up in the pulpit or out on the street. It's a strange kind of peace that unsettles as it reassures.

And there's one more thing about what Jesus means with this legacy of peace. Jesus says that this peace will be characterized by relationship with the Father and with Him. He says, "We will come to [you] and make our home with (you)." Our inheritance means allowing Jesus, who had no home, to make his home in us. It means being part of a relationship that will withstand any assault and survive any storm. This is the nature of the peace of God. And I suspect that if we are honest and just a little bit brave, we know that this is what we dearly want. St. Augustine said, "Thou hast made us for thyself and our hearts are restless till they rest in thee." That restlessness is God's offering of mysterious peace.

The peace that is our legacy, our inheritance, looks like this:

It is confident in the face of fear
It is at home wherever home is
It is sure of God's presence, though the world is falling down around us

"The peace of God, it is no peace, but strife closed in the sod. Yet let us pray for but one thing – the marvelous peace of God." *Amen*

Getting "Spiritual"

Season of Easter – John J. Capellaro

Jesus said to him, "Have I been with you all this time, Philip, and you still do not know me? Whoever has seen me has seen the Father. From now on you do know him and [you] have seen him."
John 14: 9, 7

About two years ago, an old friend of mine named Mark called me. He's a former colleague from the apparel business in New York. Mark's a terribly fashionable guy. So is his wife, Anna, who writes for the trade paper that used to be called *Women's Wear Daily*. Even their three little daughters are pretty fashionable, and I don't mean just how they dress. The whole family travels to the right places, eats at the finest restaurants on the planet, and just always seem to know what's new. Mark and I got to know each other during those intense weeks of selecting fabrics for our clothing collections, which required some very long hours together. I grew to like Mark; he seemed to know a little about a lot of different subjects, which made him interesting company. He had a wicked sense of humor, and he was wonderfully devoted to his wife and children – something I didn't often encounter in my business. So when it came time for my family and me to leave New York and head off to seminary, Mark was one of the few people with whom I could share my news. He responded to my news in two ways. He was, as always, polite, and said how happy he was for me that I'd found something that was meaningful. But then he added a little speech that was terribly fashionable. He offered his perspective thoughtfully that religion didn't hold much value for him and his family – that although it was fine for some people, he and his family were not religious people – *but* they *were* spiritual people. I left my last meeting with Mark feeling a bit depressed. There's just enough wisdom in Mark's assertions to make them attractive – and best of all, those views *are* terribly fashionable.

So when I heard from Mark a couple of years ago, it was a welcomed call, but also a surprise. After the initial courtesies were exchanged we began to get caught up about our families, given that almost ten years had passed since we'd spoken. His wife, Anna, had just been diagnosed with breast cancer and Mark just wanted someone to talk to. When I asked him about how they were dealing with things, he explained that they'd found the best doctors and were also considering a number of herbal remedies. They were doing lots of research on the web, but they couldn't escape what felt like a lack of hope that was crushing them. I asked about how they were doing spiritually, and that's when Mark let me have it. "We don't need spirituality. We need a cure. I've gone back to every self-help book on our shelves. There's nothing there that touches this! Anna has gone back to doing her Yoga, and I've done Tai-Chi for enough hours to audition for a Kung-Fu movie. Nothing touches this!"

In our subsequent conversations during these past two years, through the encouragement of some neighbors and some from me, Mark and Anna have found a church community. Anna has moved through her therapy well and seems to have a second chance at health. Their daughters have not yet attended church with their parents. They've learned early that church isn't very fashionable. But Mark and Anna are beginning their second chance together.

When I last spoke with Mark, he was calling to let me in on some discoveries he and Anna had made. He told me that there was a class at their church for people who were dealing with serious illness and there was something very "spiritual" about the things that happened in that group. He said that some people in the church had brought them meals during some of Anna's more debilitating times. He'd never experienced receiving a helping hand before – let alone from strangers. He said, "You know it felt real 'spiritual,' when those people came to see us, and drop off their macaroni and cheese casserole." He and Anna have joined a Bible study group that meets at a parishioner's house in the neighborhood, and he said, "You know I'd never heard some of those stories in the Bible, John. Do you know about that Joseph guy who donated his own tomb for Jesus to be buried in? And how about that Mary Magdalene? 'Wild on Galilee!'[1] And Peter. What a bonehead! I didn't know Jesus hung out with people like that. It's weird," he said, "but you know, Anna and I sometimes feel like we're being spoken to personally or something. Has that ever happened to you?"

Christ has met them in that church community. "I have been with you all this time, Mark and Anna. Now you begin to know me? Whoever has seen me has seen the Father. And from now on, Mark and Anna, you *do* know him and have seen him." Mark and Anna are receiving the words by which to share spiritual things that have been with them since birth. Mark and Anna's spiritual journeys have brought them to a wonderful dwelling place in God's house – or as that word actually translates from the Greek – a resting spot.[2]

Mark and Anna are discovering richness in our Christian tradition that is helping them understand their experiences of the divine. They are eager to continue to make connections between those spiritual moments of their former lives and this ancient religion called Christianity. As Mark has said, "It feels like we have always been just around the corner from God, and now with this introduction to Jesus, we somehow have turned that corner. We always knew God was there, I suppose, we just never knew how to answer."

Our good news is the fact that God is available – and perhaps most clearly in and through other people. If we're waiting for a burning bush or a voice from the sky, we may never experience God's presence. If we're waiting for a God who is only allowed into particular styles of prayer or music – we may be waiting a long time. Or perhaps worst of all, if we look for God only on Sundays, we may never find God. I admit that church may not be as fashionable as being spiritual, or as interesting as a little yoga, blended with a bit of Tai Chi, spiced with a touch of Buddhism, with an added dash of Jewish mysticism, grounded in an

---

[1] A reference to the television show, *Wild On*, which surveys trendy places to vacation for the young and beautiful.

[2] No, not *mansions*, as the old King James had it. The word *Mansion* in Old English means dwelling place not a palatial house. Bummer, I know. I much prefer the mansion idea too.

appreciation for what a swell guy that Jesus must have been. But it is a community with enough scholarship, history, story, and sacrament to sustain the hungriest of spiritually curious people.   And it is the community where we are reminded that we can know God, even when we've spent years forgetting to look. God is with us. God is with you. The Christ is present and among us. It has always been so. Alleluia. Christ is Risen. The Lord is Risen Indeed. Alleluia! From now on we know him and we have seen him.   *Amen.*

PENTECOST

A Trinity of Inclusion

Season of Pentecost, Trinity Sunday – John J. Capellaro

Indeed, God did not send the Son into the world to condemn the world, but in order that the world might be saved through him.
John 3:17

Have you noticed the moon these last few nights? Hasn't it been beautiful? Sometimes it's brilliant white; other times – a deep orange resting among colorful clouds. No wonder people have been given to moon worship over the centuries. It *is* beautiful. But as we all know, the moon is actually an ugly, lifeless rock. It has no color, vegetation, warmth, or even oxygen. It is utterly dead! Yet it's perceived beauty has inspired countless songs, poems, and dreams. The beauty and mystery that stir us as we step back from this lifeless rock comes from the sun's light which reflects from its surface.

Our scriptures are like that. In themselves they are merely a collection of manuscripts: ink on paper. Stories about another people long ago. Dead stuff. But what they can reflect is the Light of God – and the Light of the Son. To worship our scriptures is about as productive as worshipping the moon, or Moses worshipping the burning bush. But there is a beauty and mystery that can stir us, if we step back from our sacred story and experience the Son's Light reflected from the pages of our Scriptures. We lose sight of this Light when we get hung up on trying to be precise about things we cannot know, or worst of all, when we neglect to consider the context from which these stories emerge.

The passage that has been assigned to us today for Trinity Sunday is perhaps the best-known passage from the Christian Scriptures: John 3:16. How many times have we seen people holding signs at football games with "John 3:16?" Taken at a distance, there is remarkable beauty in this passage, which indeed reflects the Light of the Son.

For God so loved the world that he gave his only Son, so that everyone who believes in him may not perish, but may have eternal life.

But listen to where this passage goes: John 3:17

Indeed, God did not send the Son into the world to condemn the world, but in order that the world might be saved through him.

All right. It seems that God's interest is in the *whole* world. Verses 18 and 19:

Those who believe in him are not condemned;
but those who do not believe are condemned already,
because they have not believed in the name of the only Son of God.
And this is the judgment: that the light has come into the world,
and people loved darkness rather than light because their deeds were evil.

Translation: much, perhaps most, of humankind is doomed. Is that a message that inspires poetry, music, and hope? Or does it inspire fear? Does that reveal the Light of the Son? Or does it seem to reveal a cold, gray, dead moon? The language of John's gospel is inspiring and poetic, but it is also riddled with the language of exclusion, heavily influenced by the circumstances of his community. One scholar puts it this way: "John is obviously writing polemically and directing his fire at those who do not have '*his* faith,' which is the only correct faith."[1] In other words, whoever disagrees with John's read on things is in the dark and doomed to condemnation.

But remember that at the time John's gospel was being written, the community of John included many Jewish Christians who were being expelled from their synagogues for their beliefs. Knowing that, it's easier to understand why John's community may have had an axe to grind.

---

[1] Gerard Sloyan, *John, Interpretation. A Bible Commentary for Teaching and Preaching* (Atlanta: John Knox Press, 1988), 47.

Their experiences could not help but influence their interpretation of Jesus' message. Unfortunately, Christians have used this message of exclusion and condemnation to keep people on the outside for centuries. The tragedy of this is that the real beauty of John's gospel is often missed because we haven't stepped back to take in the whole of the story. We have decided to worship a book instead of the God whose Light is reflected from its pages.

I was working with a parishioner recently who wanted to enroll her child in one of our local Christian schools. The admissions director of the school called me to say they had a concern about this family, and wanted to ask me a couple of questions. She asked me how I would characterize the family's relationship with Jesus. It's a pretty big question, but I knew what the school was after, and so I said what I thought they wanted to hear, and then I asked what their concern was. The Director of Admissions said that following their interview of the family, the admissions committee wasn't sure if this family was saved. In the prolonged silence that followed, my tongue started to bleed. I was very, very good – until I just couldn't help myself. At the end of this awkward pause, I said, "I thought that was God's decision." That was followed with another long pause, and a simple, "Thank you for your time, Pastor Capellaro." And then "click."

It is precisely this kind of tragic ignorance and inane interpretation of scripture from which bloody persecutions are born. And even more tragic is how much the divine glory of God has been missed in these efforts to own some private key to the truth – in a way that ensures others are kept out. We need to understand the circumstances that created the hurt and anger we see coming from the community of John, and then look beyond them. Beyond the finger wagging about who's in and who's out, John has given us a remarkable blending of Greek philosophy and classic Jewish theology, which has allowed for the development of our doctrine of the Trinity. This doctrine, which has stirred Christian imaginations for centuries, is given birth in John's gospel. The message of this Doctrine is one of inclusion – not exclusion. It is a teaching about God that insists on love as a way of life – not condemnation. The doctrine of the Trinity is a poetic and inspired response to the fact of Jesus Christ. Having said that, the doctrine of the

Trinity is also a speculative statement about the nature of God, which is risky business to be sure. *"For now we see in a mirror, dimly [and we] know only in part ... (1 Corinthians 13:9)*

But what if the Christian doctrine of the Trinity is right? What if God had no beginning and has always been a self-expressing, self-communicating Being? And what if that self-expression – the Word – became flesh for an instant in history, as a gift to God's Creation? What if God's very Spirit is the very Spirit of Christ, and the defining characteristic of that Spirit is Love? If we have that right, then we must conclude that God is relational and faithful, whose essence is love. And if *we* are made in God's image, we are created with everything we need to live in harmony with one another. Our doctrine of the Trinity therefore grasps at the hope that we have the potential and responsibility to love one another – to live and to die if necessary, for the common good.

May our sacred scriptures continue to reflect the Light of the Son, so that our hunger for rigid rules is replaced with a thirst for service, love, and awe before the glory of God, which we humbly ask in the Name of the Father, and the Son, and the Holy Spirit. *Amen.*

Bigger Than All This

Season of Pentecost – Patricia R. Davis

Then the Lord answered Job out of the whirlwind: "Who is this that darkens counsel by words without knowledge?" Job 38:1

He was in the stern, asleep on the cushion; and they woke him up and said to him, "Teacher, do you not care that we are perishing?" Mark 4:38

It is a fearful thing to fall into the hands of the Living God. We have two well-known stories today in which people found themselves in mortal danger and confronted with the living God. In the first passage from the Old Testament, Job was a thoroughly good and righteous man, about as close to sinless as one can get this side of heaven. Nevertheless, he lost his children, animals, crops and servants and was reduced to sitting on a dung heap scratching at his festering skin. And, in the New Testament passage, the disciples found themselves in a terrific storm that threatened to drown them all and the one who could do something about it was apparently asleep at the wheel. Job, after a prolonged and very patient period of living with this misery, finally cries out in despair at the God who would let him be born, only to go through such heartbreak. The stories echo each other in their cries of terror and confusion: "Teacher, don't you care if we perish?" Or, in other words, "God, I'm dying here! Where are you?" We have all been there or know someone who has. And we still struggle with the hard questions. Why do such awful things happen? Why doesn't God seem to care? What about issues of justice and mercy from God at the times that it really matters? Has God simply created us and then left us to sort it out ourselves? Has God gone off somewhere to take a nap?

I meet these questions more often than I'd like. One of the people who owns a piece of my heart is a man I've come to know where I work. The child of a very troubled family, he left home at 14 and lived most of his life as a nomad, wandering the country, working at odd jobs and becoming a strong and independent man. In his early 40's now, he looks much older and is completely bedridden with rheumatoid arthritis. As if that weren't enough, he's also covered with a particularly rampant form of psoriasis, so that his whole body is covered in sores. Yet there is something compelling about him – a man of wry humor and a resigned kind of wisdom. I go to him for my lessons on surviving life. When we were talking last week, I asked him what meaning he took from all that has happened to him. He said that sometimes he thinks it's all a matter of random events in a random universe and sometimes he thinks that there's a purpose which he just can't see yet. His reasonable reply belies a desperate state that comes to many of us at some point, that place where life is simply dreadful and God doesn't seem to be at all concerned.

So we come to a passage like this one from Job. For 37 chapters Job has struggled to make sense of what has happened to him. Job has been silent while his friends blamed him and defended God, but a person can only take so much. Job finally gives up. He cries out to God, cries and screams and rants at God! He becomes "every man who ever suffered, with a kaleidoscope of conflicting emotions: he wants to die; he wants to prove he is innocent... God is his enemy; God has made a terrible mistake; God has forgotten him; or doesn't care; God will surely defend him, against God."[1] It is what the disciples will say, "Don't you care that we're drowning here?"

Now it's a dangerous thing to go yelling at God. There's just the possibility that he might answer. God might actually have something to say in response and it may not be what we're looking for. It's just possible that God will not be controlled by our concerns, that God might not see our fears in the same way that we do. And if God doesn't, if we don't get justice or healing or an end to misery, what of God then? Can He be

---

[1] *The Book of Job*, translated and with an introduction by Stephen Mitchell (San Francisco: North Point Press, 1987).

trusted when it really matters? Can God be God for us if our pain goes unresolved?

For 37 chapters, God has been silent. Now, finally, God speaks out of the whirlwind, asking a series of rhetorical questions about Job's place in the grand scheme of things. "Where were you when I laid the foundations of the earth... who shut in the sea ... made clouds its garment, and thick darkness its swaddling band?" These statements don't seem to be much of an improvement on silence. God proceeds to throw his weight around in front of this thoroughly good and blameless man like some cosmic bully. These kinds of awesome challenges have been used for centuries to beat people into abject submission, or at best a civilized acceptance of anything and everything as the "will of God." It confirms our worst fear. This isn't the God we want in our lives, a god that lords it over us and reminds us how small and worthless we are. This seems to be a god who would kick us when we're already down. As St. Theresa so famously said at one point, "With the way you treat your friends, Lord, it's no wonder you have so few of them." This isn't someone we care to be involved with.

But we are misreading Job if that is all we hear. Because this is where the divine silence is finally broken; the god who seemed to be asleep has spoken. No one can ever again accuse the Deity of aloofness, indifference, or apathy. God loves Job so much that he enters directly into a personal exchange. God's speech, while about God's greatness, is also about God's love. And Job finds himself awed but not humiliated; humbled, but not abased. Job finds himself on the threshold of a new relationship with God. From now on, their relationship will never be the same. Job has seen God at work but more importantly, Job has seen God. He has looked God in the face and lived to tell about it, heard his voice and found there an assurance that is no small comfort, but the answer to every fear.

I said before that it's a dangerous thing to go talking to God. It's also a dangerous thing to tell people that God has talked to you. They may smile and nod politely, even look very interested, but they'll quite likely go away thinking that the elevator doesn't go all the way to the top, or you're a few sandwiches short of a picnic or maybe the lights are on, but nobody's home. In other words, the message in this day and age is very clear: if you've heard God's voice, you're nuts, so keep it to yourself. But I'm coming to find that what has been recorded for ages still happens, that God does indeed talk to people today. I've learned this because some people have had the courage to tell me their stories. So I tell you mine – and then I leave for a very nice rest home somewhere!

In 1990 my husband, along with thousands of others, was deployed for what would become Operation Desert Storm. (Notice the nice parallel there: Desert Storm, storm on the sea, whirlwind?) Anyway, Rod was gone for months and we, like everyone in the country, stayed glued to the television watching and fearing a war. I grew up in the Vietnam era and the one thing I had always hoped was that our daughters wouldn't have to know war in their lifetime. War is to me a cosmic cry of pain, a great wound on the souls of men. So for months we had all prayed that God would change the hearts of men, that a way would be found to resolve the issues without the devastation of war. Well, you know what happened. No hearts were changed; the hostility and fear just escalated. War was declared, and that day I went to a service of prayer and Communion. And it seemed to me that God had abandoned ship, leaving us to make a mess of this world. The Holy Eucharist was little comfort in the face of the unthinkable evil of yet another war. So I knelt down and began to tell God how little I thought of His behavior so far. And from the midst of the storm going on inside me, I heard God say, "Remember, I am bigger than all this."

Job has shown the way for each of us. From Job, from the disciples and St. Theresa, from those who are brave enough to tell their own stories, we can learn something vitally important. We learn that we can look into the whirlwind and hear the voice of God. Then, the very response which seems to threaten us is, in fact, the answer to all our fears. Engaging in a relationship with God is always about engaging the profoundly "Other." But because it is a relationship, we are assured that the mystery of God's power is also part of the mystery of our redemption. His creative power is greater than any fear, greater than any despair, greater than anything we may dread in ourselves or in our world.

God is indeed bigger than all this.   *Thanks be to God!*

Ointment From an Alabaster Jar

Season of Pentecost – Patricia R. Davis

And a woman in the city, who was a sinner, having learned that [Jesus] was eating in the Pharisee's house, brought an alabaster jar of ointment. She stood behind him at his feet, weeping, and began to bathe his feet with her tears and to dry them with her hair. Then she continued kissing his feet and anointing them with the ointment. Luke 7:37-38

If we were to give this gospel story a different title, it might be "The Original Festival of Wine and Cheese in the Churchyard." This is a strange story within a story, and it all started with an invitation for wine and cheese in the courtyard of Simon's house. Not an unusual event since teachers and rabbis were often invited to dinner to continue the Jewish tradition of discussing just about everything. Guests would recline at the table, their feet stretched out behind them as they ate and talked. And it often happened that other people hung about the fringes to watch and listen in. It was wine and cheese in the courtyard all right, but with the addition of several local prostitutes, drug addicts and homeless people looking to pick up some good leftovers. So it was that a woman in the city, who was a sinner (that's a graceful way of saying that she was likely a prostitute), came to be there. And her behavior was nothing if not embarrassing, it was so over the top, so outrageous. The sort of thing that would be talked about the next morning over every breakfast table in town.

You've heard the story, how she made a real scene, weeping and letting down her hair in public and fawning all over Jesus as though he were the answer to her prayers. And how Simon couldn't restrain himself from commenting on such unseemly behavior, though obviously she knew little about how to properly conduct herself or she wouldn't have dared to be there at all. And how Jesus followed Simon's complaint with a story about debts being cancelled and people being grateful.

That's all well and good, but it hardly applies to real sin, does it? I mean, the woman was a sinner, but the purveyor of a victimless crime as they say – a social outcast, but hardly guilty of the kinds of things that we find *really* unforgivable. I wonder if Jesus would have had the same response if she had been a spiteful neighbor who killed your child's dog, or someone who beat her child, or murdered her husband. What if she were someone whose sins tore the very fabric of our hearts? It's much harder to talk about forgiveness and love for things like that. Those are wounds that scream to high heaven for justice, not forgiveness. And Simon, in his status and education and righteousness, was definitely interested in justice, even from a rabbi he scarcely respected. We are too, except that to insist on justice in a world that contains so little of it is to write a prescription for despair.

I find myself wishing Simon had heard this story: Among the desert Fathers there was a brother who had sinned. The Fathers spoke but Abba Pior kept silence. Later, he got up and went out; he took a sack, filled it with sand and carried it on his shoulder. He put a little sand also into a small bag which he carried in front of him. When the Fathers asked him what this meant, he said, "In this sack which contains much sand, are my sins, which are many; I have put them behind me so as not to be troubled about them and so as not to weep; and see here are the little sins of my brother which are right in front of me and I spend my time judging them. This is not right. I ought rather to carry my sins in front of me and concern myself with them, begging God to forgive me for them." The Fathers stood up and said, "Truly, this is the way of salvation."[1]

The way of salvation. But we want justice, while despair often seems the only rational response to the evil that surrounds us. We know all too

---

[1] Demetrius Dunn, *Flowers in the Desert*, p. 338.

much about the Holocaust and child abuse and sexual assault and a thousand other evils. There isn't anyone here whose personal wounds don't give them the right to scream to high heaven for justice. How can we possibly forgive and love in the face of such horror? I don't know. I wrestle with it myself. I hang on to the wrongs that have been done me and done to others. I try to use my anger to fuel a fight for more justice but I am deeply flawed and often go wrong in that struggle. Which leads me to believe that the only way we can begin to forgive others is by first carrying our own sins in front of us. We must be willing to own that we too are people with the capacity for evil, that we too are sinners, though we try like Simon to keep it hidden beneath a veneer of social niceties. We must be willing because Jesus points to this woman, this notorious sinner, as the example for us, and not the well-bred Simon who gave the party. It was in an unacceptable woman that Jesus saw something incredible, a love that grew out of her encounter with him. It's clear that she had met him before. She may have been the woman caught in adultery who was freed when none could be found to cast the first stone. Or she may have been Mary Magdalene, rumored to have been a prostitute. Whoever she was, her life was changed by her encounter with Jesus and nothing, not even the correct social norms, could stop her from expressing her gratitude for her life given back to her. Jesus points to her as our example.

A prostitute as our example. Christianity seems to get more and more ridiculous when you look at it … except that to insist on justice in a world that contains so little of it is to write a prescription for despair. If we are to escape the lure of despair, we must accept the unacceptable, forgive the unforgivable, love the unlovable. And the only way we can do that is to know that we, too, have been loved out of our sin, that we *are* this woman and we can *become* this woman. It's a choice. We can be Simon or we can be this woman. We can be Simon and look at others with judgment. We can hold on to resentments and we can nurse our grudges until we feel fully justified.

Or we can know ourselves as one more sinful person hungry for the presence of God. We can carry our sins in front of us and find ourselves loved and forgiven. I'm afraid this is one of those choices we can't escape. Our identity as Christians hinges on our willingness to know ourselves as both deeply sinful and deeply loved. It means a radical new way of being. It means acting as forgiven people. It means unfailing gratitude and the desire that everyone experience that sort of love.

And it may be that the only way someone else will experience it is through our loving them. We may be the only Jesus someone will ever see. And so I read a challenge for all of us in this story of the woman with the ointment. Every person in every church has been wounded by someone else, maybe someone sitting in a nearby pew. The wounds we bear are barely beneath the surface, rubbing a raw place and ready to bleed at the slightest additional scrape. We've been carrying *them* carefully in front of us, holding them close and protecting them. And now something about our wounds has become part and parcel of who we are, a piece of ourselves that we don't want to let go. The challenge is this: we must look at that wound. Take a look at how dear it's become, and know that there is great sin in cherishing such a thing. Being a Christian doesn't allow us this luxury. Let's make today the last day we choose to carry this particular sin. Today, let's carry our wounds, which have become our sins, to the altar. Let's finally set them down and leave them there, where the One who knows all about wounds and sin takes them to himself and forgives us. Then, in gratitude, go to the person who hurt you and offer him or her the love of God in its place. This is the challenge and the choice: to continue to love, even after we know what we know about each other. Let's make own sin be the start of our joy. Let's let the love of Christ who lives in us pour out like ointment from an alabaster jar. *Amen.*

Believe in Me

Christ the King Sunday – John J. Capellaro

"I seek not to understand so that I may believe. I seek to believe, so that I may understand." St. Anselm

Gary moved into our neighborhood from a nearby town, but to us – at age 9, he may as well have moved here from the other side of the world. His mother asked my mother if I would introduce him to some of the other boys on the block. I had to do it. She made me. I took Gary to our regular game of touch football, and obediently introduced him as the new guy on the block. Someone asked him if he knew how to play football, and he said, "Oh sure. I'm pretty good too. I can catch anything." Well – the first opportunity came, when, Billy – the best 9 year old quarterback on the whole block – let one fly right into Gary's arms – and you guessed it – he dropped it. It took all of two seconds for twelve little boys to start taunting the new kid. "Oh, I can catch anything you throw at me. Yeah right." Gary never played football with us again. It makes a difference if people believe in you or not.

Our fourth grade teacher, a fiftyish-year-old nun in the Order of The Immaculate Heart of Mary, overheard my friend Steve and me talking in the school yard during recess. Even then, Steve and I dreamed about escaping Catholic school. Our conversation was focused on what we might be when we grew up. Steve wanted to travel to far away places and write stories. Overhearing this, Sister looked down, interrupted our conversation and said, "Ah, young man, so you want to travel the world and write stories do you? And what does your father do for a living?" "He sells candy to candy stores, Sister." "And you think you're going to do better than that? I suggest you start working on your additions and

135

subtractions so you can at least get a high school diploma, and then maybe your father can get *you* a job selling candy. Travel the world and write stories ... Hah! Can you imagine?" To this day, Steve claims to be unskilled at basic arithmetic. *But* ... He's lived in Mexico, South America, and London, where he's worked as a journalist for *The Economist*. He now lives in Philadelphia with his wife of 25 years, and their two daughters, who believe in him completely. He works as a freelance writer on the political stability of foreign countries and the resulting investment climate in those places. He's also written articles for two local magazines about what it was like growing up in the Catholic school system of Philadelphia. And when he's feeling his healthiest, he writes children's stories. It's a shame that nun missed out on so much of Steve's talent – and the miracle of faith. It's remarkable how powerful it can be when people believe in you – or don't.

I left my office in the Sperry Rand building on the corner of 6th Avenue and 51st Street and stood in the late Fall cold waiting for a cab. An old friend of mine appeared next to me, who worked in the same building. He'd been a friend of mine in college – in fact he lived in the apartment next door. We'd been through a lot together. He and his wife had become good friends with Bernadette and me. It was one of those wonderful surprises when he showed up in New York in the same business and the same building I worked in. We had a history, and I trusted him. We decided to share a cab down to Grand Central, and as we took turns whistling for one, we started talking about business and our families. We hadn't seen each other in months. I hadn't told him about how involved Bernadette and I had become in our church. I didn't think he'd understand – but for some reason, it seemed like a good opportunity to let him in on something that had become very important to my family and me. He seemed a little surprised – but mostly disinterested – as if at any moment, I was going to start selling him on Jesus. I eased up on my enthusiasm just a bit – and then in the awkward pause, he looked at me in that late afternoon cold and said, "Jesus John! Next you'll be telling me, you're leaving the business to become a priest!" I had just begun the diocesan process of discernment two weeks earlier. I paused, thought for a moment, and decided to tell him the truth. "Well, actually, I *am* thinking about just that." His reaction was strong and quick. He began a tirade against "organized religion," and how anyone who got suckered into it was terribly confused, stupid, or both. I felt a distance racing between my old friend and me that hurt deeply. I began to reevaluate the values we once shared – and hold them up to the Light I'd experienced in recent years. The next several weeks were dark and sad for me – partly because my confidence about ordained ministry waned, but mostly because I wasn't sure I was ready to lose a friend this dear.

The power of belief is remarkable. So is the power of unbelief. Surely somewhere along the line we have been laughed at for our ideas or dreams – and we have experienced the power of unbelief. Surely we have laughed at others and inflicted the power of unbelief. But how often have we believed in others – believed in an idea that could not yet be touched? How often have we trusted in another person's dreams and by so doing believed that dream into reality? Isn't that what parents do for their children and friends do for one another? Isn't trust the only way love can be expressed? And isn't that trust – that belief – the vehicle for miracles?

When was the last time you believed in something invisible, and thereby participated in a miracle? Or don't you believe in miracles? When have you last believed in Jesus? Have you ever tried?

… but the leaders scoffed at him, saying, "He saved others; let him save himself if he is the Messiah of God." The soldiers also mocked him, … saying, "If you are the King of the Jews, save yourself!"

How many miracles have *we* missed in our lives? I know people who have been coming to church for years who have never even considered the possibility of believing in Jesus. I know others who *have* – even after years of numbing, safe church – and have discovered real miracles in their lives. I guess it's easier to believe in stuff we see or know. Many of us have strong beliefs in our houses, cars, and clothes. At least we can see that stuff – and find value for ourselves – not meaning – but at least some value. Others believe deeply in career. I guess we can find both value and some meaning in careers. But where life begins is to believe in what we can't see or touch – in dreams – in one another – in our invisible Christ. That's where real meaning waits.

You know, if we wait until we're clear about all the theology –If we are holding out for that airtight and clear explanation for how Buddhists, Hindus, Jews, and Muslims are incorporated into God's plan of redemption for all life – if we insist on understanding the mechanics of healing – if we must see a diagram of the machinery of salvation – before we can believe, then we'll never give ourselves the opportunity to trust. We'll never know the miracle.

As Anselm said:

"I seek not to understand so that I may believe. I seek to believe, so that I may understand."

Let's try something as an experiment this week. Why don't we try some believing? Start by believing in someone else. Kids, this is your chance: If you've ever had a dream to become an artist, an astronaut, a dancer, or anything else that is considered frivolous, and you were afraid to tell your parents – this may be your week. Give them a chance to believe in you and your dreams – however impractical they may be. And parents – let's watch our children blossom as we invest our trust and belief in them. That's an easy one.

Here's another easy one. How about a belief that might require you to do something concrete. How about believing in St. Paul's? I met a man in the parking lot the other day, who I haven't seen here in a while, and he said to me, *"When are you going to realize, John, that St. Paul's has never been a program parish and never will be. When are you going to stop talking about growth and designing programs for children. It's never going to happen."* Perhaps there might still be a few that could try believing in St. Paul's and the vision so many have had for this community for so many years – a vision that is already living and breathing.

Then move on to something harder. How about believing in ourselves again? The next time that old idea creeps into your head about who you might be – and then all those other things bombard you with doubt and self-ridicule. How about repenting of all that holds you back, and instead stick your toe in the water. Who knows? There may be someone nearby who believes in you. There may even be an invisible God who may help you through your own unbelief. Then finally, after all that practice – and all the wonderful surprises that will emerge from your belief – then perhaps – once again – try believing in Jesus. Try believing in Jesus as the image of the invisible God, as the one in whom all things hold together, as the one in whom the fullness of God is pleased to dwell, as the one who is the very foundation of your life – because if you can – if *we* can – remarkable things may happen. If you're not sure where to start – try just whispering a few dozen times a day, what the criminal on the cross said.

Hey Jesus, remember me, when you come into your kingdom.

> *Dear Jesus, remember me.*
> > *Dear Jesus, remember me.*

> > > *Sweet Lord Jesus...*
> > > > *Sweet Lord Jesus...*

Remember me?

Radical Sheep

Season of Epiphany – Patricia R. Davis

Then [Jesus] began to speak, and taught them, saying: Blessed are the poor in spirit, for theirs is the kingdom of heaven ...
Matthew 5:1-3

If you read the comics in the daily paper, then perhaps you've been following a strip called *Non-Sequitur*. Lately the strip has been dealing with the difficulty men and women have in understanding each other. In one strip the first panel features a man who hears his wife say, "You're way too stupid to be trusted driving alone in bad weather!" The next panel shows what his wife really said, which was, "Drive carefully, dear." Yet another has the man hearing, "I'm going to make you wish you were dead for the rest of the week," while his wife really said, "Tell me the truth, honey ... Do I look fat in this?" All of which is to say that what is heard is at least as dependent on the person doing the hearing as the one doing the speaking.

And I think that's at least part of the problem with the Beatitudes. We start with preconceptions and they just get compounded every time we read them. So we move farther and farther away from the truth they contain. So let's take a fresh look and try to keep our ears and minds open to what Jesus was saying and not just what we've always thought that he meant.

The Beatitudes are part of what is referred to as the Sermon on the Mount in Matthew and they're found in shorter form in Luke. If we read carefully, the first thing we discover is that, unlike the Cecil B. De Mille version, they weren't preached to a huge crowd but were spoken just to the disciples. We read that Jesus went up the mountain, sat down and *his disciples came to him.* According to Matthew, this is another occasion when Jesus pulled away from the crowds for some time alone with his disciples. And it was another in the great tradition of mountaintop teachings that began at least as far back as Noah.

According to Hebrew tradition, after Noah landed on Mount Ararat, God gave him seven laws, the first delineation of the special nature of human creation as different from the animals. Then we come to Abraham, who also went up on a mountain, to sacrifice his son Isaac. And there he learned that God cares only for the sacrifice of a broken and contrite heart. And Abraham was given some more rules for living, rules that would demonstrate their role as God's chosen people. Much later, we get Moses, who went up on a mountain where God gave him 10 laws, which were in fact the characteristics of a chosen people. It seemed pretty cut-and-dried but the Hebrews went on to explain what these 10 Commandments *really* meant in more than six hundred laws, mostly found in Leviticus. All of this, just trying to sort out what being chosen by God really means.

At any rate, Jesus followed thousands of years of history and custom and took his disciples up on a mountain and sat down with them and said, *OK, if you really want to be God's person, here's what that will look like.* And here is where we start to go off track. Because we have this picture of "gentle Jesus, meek and mild … the Good Shepherd." But what we have to hold in the front of our minds is that Jesus was talking to a group of grown men who were far from sheep. John and James were known as "the sons of thunder," not a mild description. Andrew and Peter were fishermen, a job requiring strenuous, physical labor through long hours in the hot sun. Thomas was a leader, a tower of strength who volunteered to go with Jesus to his death, a man whose courage allowed him to express doubt. All of which leads me to believe that if we think these Beatitudes are about submissive, being content-with-your-lot kind of behavior, we've got another think coming. I believe that these sayings, if we have ears to hear, call for an active engagement with life, for a partnership of strength and weakness, and for strength made perfect in weakness.

Consider the vocabulary. *Blessed are the poor in spirit.* Poor in spirit has been taken to mean downtrodden and lacking any sense of self. But *poor in spirit* can mean someone without pretension, someone aware of the difference between God's image of perfection and human reality. So someone who is *poor in spirit* is dependent all right, dependant upon the grace of God and so has a glimpse of the kingdom of heaven. Those who *mourn* ... Are they the people who are always sad and always bemoaning the sad state of the world or are they the people who are grieved by the distance between God and self and yearn to bridge the distance? And then we come to *meek*. We hear *meek* and we think of a mouse, or a sheep, someone content to go along to get along, letting someone else lead. But *meek* simply means someone who is gentle and courteous, free from self-will and unresentful. And that's a trait that takes work! And *merciful*. That can be heard as willing to be stepped on, as willing to offer forgiveness without the work of repentance. But mercy, like the mercy of God, is an active compassion for others that refuses to claim its own power. And not to belabor the point, but a *peacemaker* has been interpreted as a namby-pamby sort of person willing to do anything to avoid a quarrel. But in reality, a *peacemaker* is someone who deliberately goes where the conflict is in order to bring about reconciliation. I just don't hear any sheep-like behavior here. What I hear are some powerful lessons given to some powerful men about how that power might be put to good use as God's people actively engaged with the world.

So, like the stereotypical husband-wife dialogue in the comics, the Beatitudes are both straightforward and unbelievably complex. I believe they challenge us to behavior which is far from meek and mild, not at all compliant, but rather courageous and daring. They call for an approach to life that is open-eyed and brave, because being this kind of person, God's person, is not for the timid of mind or heart. It means keeping always in mind the gulf between our lives and God's vision. It means refusing to put ourselves first in a world that recognizes only position and power. It means forgiving out of compassion instead of out of a need to feel bigger and better than. It means wading into conflict and giving all we've got to resolve that conflict. These are the things that will bring a glimpse into the mind of God, a little bit of the kingdom of heaven here and now.

So how might we reframe the Beatitudes so that we can hear them as they were meant, as a call to radical living? Perhaps they might sound like:

Blessed are the discontented, for they know that this life is not everything, but that God is.

Blessed are those who are saddened by the same things that sadden the heart of God, for they will be moved to change the world.

Blessed are those who refuse to put themselves first, for they honor the soul of God in those around them.

Blessed are the dissatisfied, for they refuse to accept what is for that which can be.

Blessed are those who go where there is trouble, for they know that someday love will finally and forever defeat evil.

Blessed are those who know that peace of mind is not the same as the peace of God, for the peace of God does not make life easy but makes life able to be lived creatively in the midst of trouble.

Blessed are those who live bravely with despair, discouragement and defeat, for they will discover that God still lives and moves among us and they will be his partners in creation.

Amen.

Prophets Everywhere!

Season of Pentecost – Patricia R. Davis

On the sabbath [Jesus] began to teach in the synagogue, and many who heard him were astounded. They said, "Where did this man get all this?" Mark 6:2

There are prophets everywhere! While in first century Israel the orthodox position was that prophecy had ceased with the destruction of the first Temple, there were indeed prophets everywhere. So when Jesus came along acting out the will of God in a living parable, it was perhaps to be expected that he would receive a lukewarm reception by some of the more cynical in the country. And while he never held himself up as a prophet, the reception he received from his hometown had to be disheartening. Jesus arrived there, the memory of raising Jairus' daughter fresh in his mind, and he began to teach in the synagogue. We might think that his miracles would have given him a reputation to be reckoned with, at least something on the order of a headline in the local paper saying, "Local Boy Makes Good." But the townspeople, the friends and neighbors of his childhood, could scarcely contain themselves. It's as though Jesus has trespassed some unwritten code; he's crossed the line now and forgotten who he is. But *they* know him and have no qualms about reminding him who he is. "Isn't this the carpenter, the son of Mary ... ?" This is Jesus, the child of a shotgun wedding, the boy they watched grow up, their children's playmate, and they are so familiar with him that they can't see that he could have become anyone different than the child they once knew. For them, he will always be Mary's son. It's in this context that Jesus makes the now famous comment about a prophet being without honor in his own country.

144

Now I don't believe that Jesus cared about honor for himself or the approval of others but he did make this remark. So it's an analogy that bears investigation. And it contains a truth so unremarkable that we seldom even think about it. That is, that we rely on things and people staying the same; in fact, we count on it for our own feeling of security. So that when we are familiar with someone or something, we can cease to really see them. Something in us goes deaf, dumb and blind and we see only what we expect to see. It's a bit like going back for a class reunion and hearing, "Why, you haven't changed a bit!" What's meant as a compliment is really a condemnation to eternal sameness. It doesn't allow for growth and change, doesn't allow that life and God change us in ways that may be surprising and a little uncomfortable.

But ... God is a living God, not content with the status quo, not content to let us rest on our laurels, so he keeps calling us to new life, keeps sending Jesus and his prophets into our proverbial hometown and he uses the most ordinary people in the most ordinary places. Now the task of a prophet is straightforward, if not always simple: prophets proclaim the will of God, much as Jesus did in his ministry. Prophets call us to look at what is and see what could be, if seen through the mind of God. Consider these prophets:

The first Episcopal priest that I knew said something unusual during our instruction for Confirmation. This priest said that when we approach the Bishop for the rite, we are to give him only our first name. He said that this is because God doesn't call us to be his people because we are the son or daughter of so-and-so or because we can claim a stellar family tree, but because we are his own, marked as his own even, at Baptism. In other words God calls us by our given name, and we all have one last name, which is *Christian*. Prophetic? You bet! From that day on, a whole new vision of who I might be opened up, along with a yearning to know who this person is that God has in mind for me to become. An absolutely prophetic experience.

Or consider this one: We were on vacation at the beach when I saw a very young prophet in action. For 14 years now we've held a family reunion at the beach and each year our 2 daughters have built some kind of sand sculpture. They were simple at first, sand castles with varying turrets and towers, getting a bit more complicated as our girls grew.

Then they branched out and we were treated to an octopus one year and another year, a sea monster with just humps showing above the waves. Once they made a large dragon guarding a treasure chest. This year it was a life-sized mermaid stretched out on the sand. She had long flowing hair and the scales on her tail fin were individually crafted. She wore a necklace of seashells and a seashell ring on her finger. It takes several hours to craft a sand sculpture like this so the girls started at low tide. When they were finished we went up to the house for lunch and a nap and then went back down to the beach about 4 o'clock to get one last look at her before the tide came in. That's pretty much our routine but it doesn't always work. Sometimes we go down and someone has been there before us and stomped the sculpture into a discouraging mess, and all the beauty's gone out of it. But this time when we went down, she was still there, unharmed, and a little boy, about 3 years old, was sitting in front of her, between the mermaid and the incoming sea. The water was just beginning to lap at the edges of her scales and every time a bit of sand broke away, the little boy would pat it back into place. Soon two small friends joined him and as the waves kept coming, they kept trying to protect her from the coming destruction. There was a small group of grownups standing by, some of them commenting on the futility of trying to hold back the ocean. But one of the women told us how she had seen the sculpture on her morning bike ride and ridden all the way back home to tell the rest of her family to come and see.

There were actually prophets all over the beach that afternoon. There was the little boy who acted out a beautiful parable about what it can mean to be part of a world in which good things and people are often assaulted and saving them seems like a futile effort. He taught us how easy it is to get help when others can see that it's needed and someone shows the way. The grownups that laughed at his efforts taught us how easy it is to become apathetic when the task seems overwhelming. And the woman who went back to get her friends taught us about sharing wonder with others.

Or consider this prophet: On Monday I stopped in to visit a woman with Alzheimer's disease. She was very upset, almost distraught. What she said brought me up short and left me stunned. What she said was, *I seem to have lost myself somewhere. Is there anyone here who can help me find myself?* In her confusion was a great wisdom. She knew what most of us seldom realize: that we can lose ourselves and be too busy to notice.

Since the destruction of the Temple, *prophecy is said to be found only in the utterances of fools and children.* We could find ourselves in worse company than these.

But we have a choice when God sends his prophets into our lives. We can miss them altogether because we think we know who they are and what they're about. We can encourage others to ignore these prophets too, making fun of them if they seem to see something that we don't. And there is a third choice. We can be aware that there are prophets everywhere. We can remain open to the possibility that God is still acting in the most ordinary of people and events. Because the great danger is not that we won't recognize Christ coming into our lives because he's a stranger ... but because he's a friend. *Amen.*

Holy Imagination, Batman!

Transfiguration Sunday – John J. Capellaro

While he was still speaking, suddenly a bright cloud overshadowed them, and from the cloud a voice said, "This is my Son, the Beloved; with him I am well pleased; listen to him!" When the disciples heard this, they fell to the ground and were overcome by fear. Matthew 17:5-6

Jesus and three of his friends ascend a mountain so Jesus may pray. While he prays, just as in the Garden of Gethsemane, his friends fall asleep. And then suddenly they are stirred from their sleep. Something is taking place while their friend and teacher prays. We don't know if a sound arouses them – or a smell – a change in temperature – a sudden light – but something causes them to awaken, and they believe they see Jesus alongside Moses and Elijah. And Jesus' face has changed. It seems to be shining – not unlike the stories these men had heard since childhood about how Moses' face glowed after he'd been in the company of God. Jesus is in conversation with Elijah and Moses, and they are talking about his trek to Jerusalem – the one that James, Peter, and John, don't want to hear about. Peter mutters something about setting up tents for their mystical guests, and as he does all are hushed as a cloud envelops them. And then from the cloud all three men hear a voice. They hear it clear as can be. *"This is my Son, my Chosen; listen to him!"* And then – it is over. As quickly as it started – it is over. And the lives of these men were never the same.

Can you imagine it? Will we allow ourselves to consider the possibility? One commentator writes about this passage:

For a brief moment the curtain was drawn aside and the disciples have been allowed to see in Jesus something of the Glory of God – of that other life to which we are normally blind.[1]

What other life? Is there such a thing? And if there is – can we catch glimpses? When was the last time your imagination was captured so fully that your life was forever changed?

I have a friend named Alex who told me a story once about a time he was in church after *not* being in church for many years. A crucifer led the procession. Alex was standing in the back of the church not feeling welcomed enough or perhaps worthy enough to be in a pew. As the crucifer passed one of the church windows, the sun reflected off the cross so powerfully that Alex says a ball of light left the cross, flew across the room and hit him in the chest. He felt heat, he felt awe, and he felt peace. Alex has what Thomas Moore calls a *"Holy Imagination,"*[2] which is exactly what it takes to perceive the Glory of God.

How healthy is your "Holy Imagination?" Does it get much exercise? "As we 'grow up,' we get sophisticated [and grow] out of our 'Holy Imaginations'… becoming too smart about the things that cause children to wonder."[3] We miss "the musical nature of reality,"[4] and the Glory of God. And you don't need to be in Church to use a Holy Imagination or perceive God's Glory. The wonder and Mystery of God is evident in all the world – and on occasion even in church.

Have you ever noticed how a pregnant person glows? Look carefully next time. Have you ever experienced a sensation of heat during prayer and the laying on of hands? I know a young man who just a few short months ago fell in love. Suddenly he sees the world in a new way and is now infused with an otherworldly value. The change is so dramatic that

---

[1] Paraphrase of comment by Eduard Schweizer's *The Good News According to Luke*, 161.
[2] Thomas Moore, *The Re-Enchantment of Everyday Life* (New York, New York: HarperCollins, 1996), x.
[3] Ibid, xvi.
[4] Ibid, 218.

old ways of thinking – old ways of living – no longer work. His imagination has been so stirred that his life is forever changed. It takes a Holy Imagination to fall in love.

Our religion is not about proving or believing in the Transfiguration of Christ – or any other mystery for that matter. It is about allowing our Holy Imaginations to breathe sufficiently to allow the Glory of God to permeate our lives. *A religion reduced to belief is useless.* In such a religion there is no place for an open-minded appreciation of the world's sacredness. In such a religion we are required to shut down our Holy Imaginations. Following Christ is not about clarifying what we believe or selecting pieces of the tradition that can be reasonably explained. It is about sitting in silence before the great possibility of hope – and learning to live in that midrealm where *imagination is taken seriously but not literally* – where mystery and wonder have as much value as understanding. There is a vision of God's glory that awaits us. Will we allow ourselves to see? Will we allow ourselves to be loved – perhaps even healed? Will we allow ourselves to hear the words?

> *Then from the cloud came a voice that said,*
> *"This is my Son, my Chosen; listen to him!"*   Amen.

Us and Them and Grace In Between

Season of Pentecost – Patricia R. Davis

But the Lord is with me like a dread warrior; therefore my persecutors will stumble, and they will not prevail. They will be greatly shamed, for they will not succeed ... let me see your retribution upon them, for to you I have committed my cause.
Jeremiah 20:7-13

Surely, for your sake have I suffered reproach,
    And shame has covered my face.
I have become a stranger to my own kindred,
    An alien to my mother's children.   Psalm 69:8-9

See, I am sending you out like sheep into the midst of wolves; so be wise as serpents and innocent as doves. Beware of them, for they will hand you over to councils and flog you in their synagogues ...
Matthew 10:16-17

Once upon a time a group of old, tired priests sat around a long conference table, selecting passages of scripture to be read throughout the year. They'd made their way through Advent, Christmas, Epiphany, Lent, Easter and Pentecost. Weary now, and having used up all their favorite stories, they still had to find material for reading and preaching that would get the church through the summer. And maybe the summer heat was getting to them a bit, too. Because a mood of sadistic irony came upon them. "Well," they said. "These preachers have had it far too easy up to now with all those wonderful stories and great parables. It's time they had to struggle a bit; maybe it will keep everyone awake and listening when they'd rather be dozing on the beach. So, let's give them some passages guaranteed to make everyone sit up and take notice." And that's how we got today's lessons, or at least that's how it could have happened.

And these lessons are difficult. Jeremiah, the Psalmist and the writer of Matthew all talk about being threatened and assaulted, alienated from their communities and feeling full of fear. With the exception of that bit about the sparrows, there's very little in today's lessons that is reassuring. The language is that of "us" and "them." This is fighting language and it doesn't sound anything like the comfortable words we're used to hearing. And in a world that has far too much of "us" and "them," this isn't what we want to dwell on, the reality of human hatred and persecution. Far better to hold up the ideal of brotherly love on a Sunday morning, of peace and good will toward men, than give credence to human evil. That's the Jesus we know and love.

But the reality is that Jesus did have some rather harsh words on occasion, though this lesson from Matthew probably doesn't reflect his words at this time and place. This is post-Easter language, the language of a church in trouble. It's likely that these words came out of the persecutions of the early church and are read back into the story to give strength and encouragement to believers. But Jesus did spell out early and often the cost of discipleship. Remember *If anyone comes to me and does not hate father and mother, wife and children, brothers and sisters, even his own life, he cannot be my disciple?* Remember *Do you think that I have come to bring peace? ... No, I tell you, but rather division!* Remember James and John, called to leave their father and mother to follow Jesus? Jesus called others to forget about burying their dead, to leave home and family and way of life, all to follow him and put him first. Do we imagine that there was no family alienation, that there were no angry words, no disinheritance, and no threat of death in obeying Jesus? We must not underestimate the cost of being a Christian because the stark truth is that being a Christian may make "us" and "them" a painful reality. What we do with that reality reveals who it is we really follow. Let me illustrate with stories.

She was the wife of a priest in an old and historic parish. With a beautiful bevy of daughters, she had her hands full as it was. But her girls needed a preschool and so did the many families that she and her husband met as they went about the community, so she started a preschool at the church. It was a lovely idea until the parishioners learned that it was to be open to "them," including scholarships for those who couldn't afford to attend school in such fine surroundings. But she stood up for Christ, and it cost her.

Much, much later, when her husband had retired as priest and she might have been expected to look to a quieter life, she became involved with a small group of people trying to make a difference in the inner city. She started out helping with worship services but soon was counseling girls who found themselves pregnant, going to court with mothers as they watched their sons sent away to prison, meeting with teenagers who saw their friends gunned down in drive-by shootings. One day, while giving a young black man a ride home, she was stopped by the police. They wanted to know where she was going and what she was doing. *Was this young man in her car by her invitation?* When word reached the Bishop, he called her in. *You need some protection,* he said. *I think you should be ordained. At least the collar may explain what it is you're doing in that part of town.* And her daughters were appalled. If the Bishop thought it wasn't safe, how could she continue to risk her life, to risk being taken away from them? Hadn't she done enough in one lifetime to help "them"? It's time to quit all this and let someone else take up the cross. It was the great grief of her heart, that "they" couldn't understand this call to make Christ known in the places where He was most needed. But she <u>was</u> ordained and continues to serve the inner city, going where most of us dread to go. It is at tremendous cost.

Christian X was king of Denmark, but that power meant nothing when Germany invaded in 1940. The Germans allowed him to remain in office as long as he obeyed their demands. Among the first was that he issue an edict instructing all Jews in Denmark to wear the Star of David prominently displayed on their clothing. "They" were a people marked as less than human and not entitled to the same rights as others. So Christian issued the edict and then appeared the next day wearing the Star of David himself. Inspired by his example, soon the entire population of Denmark wore the Star of David. The Danes went on to develop numerous resistance groups which eroded the armor of the German military and resulted in the successful evacuation of almost all of Denmark's Jews, about 7000 people. But King Christian paid a price for his actions: he was imprisoned from 1943-45 and died 2 years later.

In these stories we have a glimpse of the costly grace described by Dietrich Bonhoeffer. It's the grace that comes from carrying the cross and following Christ. I quote Bonhoeffer: *Costly grace is the treasure hidden in the fields. For the sake of it, a man will gladly sell all that he has. It is the pearl of great price for which the merchant will sell all his goods. It is a call of Christ at which the disciple leaves his nets and follows him. It is costly because it costs a man his life; it is grace because it gives a man his only true life.* It may be that the grace of God doesn't bring us in conflict with our family, our community, our job or our friends, but then again, it may. It may be that we are called to make the hard decisions, to stand up when it would be easier to lie down. It may be that we are misunderstood, attacked verbally or physically, shut out or shut up in prison, perhaps even have to die for his amazing grace. It may be that it really is "us" and "them."

Sometimes it is necessary to use that language, to name the evil. But when we do so, it should be accompanied by tremendous sadness. If a secret glee sneaks in, if we find ourselves taking pride in being "us," then we have laid down the cross and picked up something much worse. Us and them language must never be the last word of a Christian. Because, even with Jesus' words about the pain and strife involved in following him, the dream of God is a people where there is no "us" and "them" but only and always "us." That is the clear lesson of Jesus' time among us, the meaning of his final forgiving words on the cross, and the ultimate gift of His costly grace.

The language of "us" and "them" may be a reality but it should always be a reality that we are uncomfortable with. As Christians, we must always grieve such language and the evil that evokes it. We must yearn and hope and pray that such language never makes a home in our hearts. The words of the Christian Gospel can be used to describe a reality that is, or they can be used to create a reality that should never be. The difference is critical. *Amen (Let it be so)*.

Rowing Like Mad

Season of Pentecost – Patricia R. Davis

Immediately after the feeding of the five thousand, Jesus made his disciples get into the boat and go on ahead to the other side, to Bethsaida, while he dismissed the crowd ... When evening came, the boat was out on the sea, and [Jesus] was alone on the land. When he saw that they were straining at the oars against an adverse wind, he came towards them early in the morning, walking on the sea. He intended to pass them by. But when they saw him walking on the sea, they thought it was a ghost and cried out; for they all saw him and were terrified. But immediately he spoke to them and said, "Take heart, it is I; do not be afraid." Then he got into the boat with them and the wind ceased. And they were utterly astounded, for they did not understand about the loaves, but their hearts were hardened.   Mark 6:45-52

What a very curious way to end a story! "... they did not understand about the loaves, but their hearts were hardened."

Now I confess that I don't care for the Gospel of Mark as much as the others, particularly John, the Bach of the Gospels, with its soaring language and developed theology. With Mark, what you see is what you get. Mark is all "right away" and "immediately" and one thing follows another so quickly that we barely have time to absorb one story before we're thrown into another. Which may be the point. Mark was writing to a community of Christians under threat of persecution and facing possible martyrdom. It was imperative that his message of salvation by the courageous self-giving of Jesus be received and understood in order to build up the spiritual strength of the believers. The urgency and importance comes through in every phrase so that we are left breathless, like so many men rowing a boat against the wind.

Or, it may be that life with Jesus often felt like that, tearing from one town to another, healing and preaching as though time were running out. Today's story follows, you may remember, Jesus' sending the disciples out to try their hands at preaching and healing on their own. As soon as they returned, they spent the day trying to shepherd a crowd of 5000, and then rustle up dinner for all these people with the supplies at hand. Facing a severe strain on the family finances, they all but gave up in despair. But they made it through that and no sooner had the supper dishes been cleared away than Jesus ushered them into a boat and sent them on ahead, presumably to get things ready in the next town. So now they're rowing like mad, and it's dark as can be and it's 3 or 4 in the morning and they're bone tired and here comes Jesus, and it looks like he's going to pass right by. Sound familiar? It's no wonder they didn't understand about the loaves. They hadn't had time to sit and breathe, much less process all that had been happening.

And this is most of us, most of the time, moving from one task to another, from one crisis to another, trying to make it through the day so that we can get to bed, sleep a little, get up and start all over again. We want to lead lives worthy of our calling as God's children, we want to lead lives filled with *humility and gentleness, with patience, bearing with one another in love, making every effort to maintain the unity of Spirit in the bond of peace,* but we're so busy! We can hear that passage from Ephesians and simply hear a list of chores, all that teaching and equipping and building, until being a child of God can feel like one more task to be accomplished. It's no wonder we feel "tossed to and fro and blown about!"

Now there are two great dangers in the busy life that we lead. The first is that we can mistake our busyness for our salvation. That is, we can come to believe that rowing the boat is actually getting us someplace, that someplace being the front gate of heaven. We like to believe that what we do has some greater purpose, that maybe, really, God needs our help to work out our salvation and usher in the kingdom. So we spend our days striving always and everywhere to prove that we are worthy, by what we accomplish, of being in charge of the boat of our lives. And we become the disciples, exhausted but still rowing like mad, thinking we have to get everything ready for Jesus to come. We're doing this when we're too busy with work to take a walk around the block with our spouse. We're doing this when we're too tired from all our important tasks to step outside and look at the fireflies on a summer evening. We're doing this when we define ourselves by salary, position or title and none of those include "child of God." In all these things, we're rowing like mad and thinking we're actually getting someplace. But then one day, if we're lucky, we glance up from our rowing and find, to our dismay, that God doesn't even need our boat and is, in fact, making great strides in rough seas without our help at all!

The second danger is more subtle and somewhat like the first. The second danger is that we may mistake our busyness for life itself; in other words, that we may come to think that rowing the boat is all there is. I saw a bumper sticker the other day that made me sad. Now I generally think bumper stickers are interesting. It's fascinating to see what sentiments people will display on their car. This one said, "Life is hard, then you die." That's the feeling that can sneak in and settle in our hearts when we substitute staying busy for a relationship with the One who sends us out in the first place. We can hit the floor running in the morning, scanning the Day-timer or Palm Pilot to see what's on the agenda, and neglect to invite the One who gives us that day to be part of it. So it is that we sit in church wondering why there are all these long silent spaces … couldn't we just move the service along a little bit? After all, we have to get home and get lunch and get through a list of errands and chores before Monday morning rolls around again. We even feel it coming up to the rail for communion, that pressure to keep the line moving, there are others waiting so, for goodness' sake, don't dawdle at the rail to actually pray! It's incredible the things we do and the ways that our hearts can be hardened without our even knowing it.

The renowned preacher Phillips Brooks said it well when he said, "The great danger facing all of us – let me say it again, for one feels it tremendously – is not that we shall make an absolute failure of life, nor that we shall fall into outright viciousness, nor that we shall be terribly unhappy, nor that we shall feel that life has no meaning at all – not these things. The danger is that we may fail to perceive life's greatest meaning, fall short of its highest good, miss its deepest and most abiding happiness, be unable to render the most needed service, be unconscious of life ablaze with the light of the Presence of God – and be content to have it so – that is the danger. That some day we may wake up and find that we have always been busy with the husks and trappings of life – and have really missed life itself. For life without God, to one who has known the richness and joy of life with him, is unthinkable, impossible. That is what one prays one's friends may be spared – satisfaction with a life that falls short of the best, that has no tingle and thrill which comes from a friendship with the Father."

But there is a third possibility. It's just possible that when we find ourselves rowing into a headwind, that wind is the breath of God blowing over our sea, ruffling the water. That brooding Spirit of God which was present at creation seeks to do a creative work in us. So the Spirit of God makes us slow down, seeks to stir up our souls, calls us to struggle less and watch for Jesus striding across the water to join us.

Ultimately, what made the disciples memorable people was not their preaching or healing or rowing all over the place, but their friendship with the man called Jesus. It was that living relationship that caused the message to spread and grow and cover the earth with its joy. Our faith is, at the last, the story of a friendship that changes all the rowing into joy. *Amen.*

The Outsiders

Season of Pentecost – John J. Capellaro

Then one of them, when he saw that he was healed, turned back, praising God with a loud voice. He prostrated himself at Jesus' feet and thanked him. And he was a Samaritan. Luke 17:15-16

Elimelech (which means "My God is King") and his wife, Naomi (which means "Pleasant") live in Bethlehem (which means "Place of Food.") They have two sons: Mahlon (which means "Weak") and Chilion (which means "Sickly"). *(We may have a hint as to where this story is going.)* "My God is King" and his wife, "Pleasant," take their two children "Weak" and "Sickly" and leave their hometown, "place of food," because there is no food. They move to Moab, which *is* a place of food, although not called that, because it was called Moab, which doesn't mean anything as far as I can find out – other than an area which was settled by Moab, who was the son of Lot and one of his own daughters. But that's another story. They move there temporarily, but as things sometimes happen, time gets away from them, and "Weak" and "Sickly" grow up. While living in Moab, both boys marry non-Jewish, foreign Moabite women. One is named Orpah, which means "Rain Cloud," and the other is named Ruth, which means "Friend."

So we now have "My God is King," "Pleasant," their two sons, "Weak," and "Sickly," and their Moabite daughters-in-law, "Rain Cloud" and "Friend." My God is King becomes ill and dies. Then – surprise! surprise! – "Weak," and "Sickly" die. We now have "Pleasant," "Rain Cloud," and "Friend," on their own without husbands or any means of support. Pleasant, who is now feeling anything but, decides to head back to "Place of Food" – you know, Bethlehem. But because she cannot care for her non-Jewish, Moabite, daughters-in-law, she attempts to send them

159

off, so they may return to their people, and she may return to her people. Rain Cloud agrees to leave, but "Friend" (Ruth), insists on staying with Pleasant – who now wants to be called "Bitter." Bitter (formerly Pleasant) says to Friend, "Turn back, my daughter, go your way, for I am too old to have a husband ... it has been far more bitter for me than for you, because the hand of the LORD has turned against me." But "Friend"/Ruth remains steadfast and says, "Do not press me to leave you ... Where you go, I will go; your people shall be my people, and your God my God. Where you die, I will die – there will I be buried."

We see in Ruth, this aptly named "Friend," a person who chooses trust. Ruth is not embittered by her misfortune, but rather offers commitment to a woman whom she may love, but who cannot provide a future. Ruth chooses to cling, not to a past, but to a present, not to a male, but to a female for whom *she* will provide protection and support, and chooses to trust in a God who has so far demonstrated very little to warrant that trust. Our Hebrew Scriptures hold up for us an outsider, as the epitome of faithful behavior. And it is this outsider, this Moabite woman, who will later bear a son who will be grandfather to King David himself.

As Jesus moves towards his demise in Jerusalem, ten people afflicted with leprosy approach him. They call out saying, *"Jesus, Master, have mercy on us."* Jesus offers no word of healing, no touch – but simply asks them to go show themselves to the priests, which is required by Jewish Law if a leper is healed. Jesus treats the lepers as already healed, and in their obedient response to go see the priests, the healings take place. One of the ten turns back, however, "praising God with a loud voice. He prostrates himself at Jesus' feet and thanks him. And he is a Samaritan." Luke's story is meant to convey not so much the importance of good manners, but rather whom Jesus selects as an example of faithful behavior – and how he responds to that behavior. The one who returns, bellowing his praises, and falling at Jesus' feet is again – an outsider. He is an outsider because of his leprosy, but more significantly, an outsider because he is a Samaritan, a person with Jewish roots whose particular brand of Judaism was considered heretical among mainstream Jews. As this Samaritan falls at his Jesus' feet, our Lord says to him, "Your faith has made you well." According to several scholars however, a better translation of those words is, "Your faith has saved you."   By his acknowledgment of Jesus as God's agent of healing, he is no longer an outsider, but *is* among the chosen. His expression of trust in Jesus – his hollers of praise for the one whose presence reflects God – places him among the chosen.   Once again, an outsider shows us what faithful behavior looks like.

The model of faith we're given in these outsiders isn't so much a faith that's big or deeply rooted. It is *not* well reasoned, or a faith that can be measured.   It's just simple trust: trust in the face of being uncertain, trust in the face of disappointment or even despair. This trust or faith is something we either do – or we don't do. What we say we believe from one moment in our life to the next is not really what's important. It's about living and moving in trust. It's about choosing to trust, even in the face of disappointment, in the face of that which separates us from the world, in the face of that which damages our belonging. It's about embracing the "outsiderness" in us as the thing that invites relationship with God.

Ruth's decision to trust in her mother-in-law and in God was its own reward: a noble and honorable gesture of trust without promise of a better life. The Samaritan leper's choice to return and offer thanks was its own reward: a noble and honorable gesture without promise of anything more than the healing already granted. Perhaps Ruth and the leper knew more about their "outsiderness" than most others; perhaps that's why they are moved to trust more fully and be examples and agents of Grace; perhaps it's people like Ruth and the leper who know about what being an outsider really means who are more apt to fall on their faces and offer their cries of praise and thanks. It's not that God likes outsiders better. I don't know who or how God likes or loves – that's why God is God and we're not. It just seems that as soon as we think of ourselves as *insiders*, we're getting into dangerous waters. I suppose it's our "outsiderness" that keeps us within God's reach.

So to the extent that you are an outsider, that I am an outsider, we might count our blessings. And the good news is – we don't have to be a leper, a Samaritan, a Moabite widow – or anything else special to be an outsider. I think most of us already are. I know some military families who have their own special anxieties that the rest of us can't fully appreciate. They are, in many ways, outsiders. I know folks who have been coming to this church for years, who have told me that as they look around and see so many new faces, although they love seeing their church grow, they also sometimes feel like outsiders in their own church. There are others who are out of work in this church who, when asked the ultimate question, "Oh and what do you do?" become outsiders -- however they answer the question. We have several among us who are battling serious illness who can no longer participate in their community as they used to. We're all outsiders in one way or another, and most of us can't stand our "outsiderness." Well, God can. And God does. It's the thing that keeps us within God's reach. If we don't become embittered by our isolation, it's the thing that draws us to God and God to us – and invites us all to cry out in trust, *"Jesus, Master have mercy on us!"* Amen.

Life Flight

Season of Pentecost – Patricia R. Davis

But God said to him, "You fool! This very night your life is being demanded of you. And the things you have prepared, whose will they be?" Luke 12:20

Airplane travel can be really enlightening if we're halfway paying attention. On an airplane the flight attendants make a whole slew of announcements designed to minimize risk. Part of it goes like this: *Please take a moment to locate the exit nearest to you. Be aware that the nearest usable exit may be located behind you.* That's good advice for us, folks. Take time right now to locate the nearest usable exit because these lessons certainly make us want to run for it!

The lessons for today contain some heavy baggage and they promise a trip that isn't just a vacation. It looks like we have to talk about either money or dying, neither one of which is appropriate for polite company, and they are guaranteed to get the preacher in trouble. Just listen to these announcements:

First, from Ecclesiastes: *I saw all the deeds that are done under the sun; and see, all is vanity and chasing after wind ... For all their days are full of pain, and their work is a vexation; even at night their minds do not rest.* (Ecclesiastes 1:12-14; 2:1-23) Feel familiar? Even given that the writer was probably suffering from clinical depression, these are tough ideas. They're some we've all probably secretly harbored at some time in our lives, those times when we want to turn and give our hearts up to despair.

So then we move on, looking for some better news from the early Christians and we get this veritable checklist of awfulness from Paul: *Put to death fornication, impurity, passion, evil desire, and greed ... You must get rid of all such things – anger, wrath, malice, slander and abusive language from your mouth.* (Colossians 3:5-17) And we know he's not just making this all up; these are behaviors he's seen in his Christian companions, his fellow passengers on Earth Airlines. It's all rather discouraging.

So we move on to Luke. And here we find Jesus telling a parable about a man who works hard and *succeeds*. And just when things are really comfortable and he can finally relax and stop trying so hard, he hears God say, *You fool!* Now when we hear God say, *You fool!* we can be sure that what comes next isn't going to be good! This man who has done so well and achieved so much is going to die without ever enjoying it all. It sounds like the writer of Ecclesiastes was right. It's all vanity and chasing after wind. Right about now I'm ready to head for the nearest exit and get off this plane! So let's change the subject.

It's an interesting thing to meet people when they come into a nursing home. Many come from the hospital and so they come with only the clothes on their backs and a few toiletries they were given. And if I talk to them in these first few days, the most common feeling is one of loss, of everything that has been left behind or given up. But the longer they stay, the more stuff seems to accumulate. First come pictures from home and maybe a favorite armchair for the corner. Then come stuffed animals and cross-stitch plaques and little figurines and a bedside table crammed with lotions and creams, candy and crackers.

Pretty soon the closet is crammed with clothes for summer and winter, though the temperature is constant inside, and by this time, two people can barely move for all the stuff in the room. It's one of those unwritten laws, "Stuff expands to fill the available space." This is the way it usually goes. But some people never get beyond the family pictures and a pot of flowers in the window. Their rooms stay plain and rather bare, rather like Thoreau at Walden Pond. They've pared things down to what matters, what is essential for this part of the trip. Both are ways of coping with aging and illness and a world turned upside down, and ways of saying what's important.

But it's so hard to let go of our stuff. It's so hard not to keep collecting things, keep wanting things. Personally, I have this theory that I won't die until all my books are read. And at the rate I keep buying books, I figure I'm good for another hundred years!   But there comes a moment of truth, the moment when the ground comes rushing up at us like a plane crash, and we know that none of it will protect us from what we fear.

Perhaps it comes after months and years of contemplating divorce. The reality that the marriage is really over finally dawns and we stand in the kitchen and look at the accumulation of our union and realize that none of it is important without a relationship to give it meaning. Perhaps it comes with a child's serious illness, those hours spent by the hospital bed, when we would trade all that we have and all that we've done and all that we are for our child, well and happy again. Perhaps it comes on a Navy ship, far out at sea. The realization that who and what holds our heart is something else altogether different from rank and achievement. Perhaps it comes when a spouse dies and what looked like things to make our lives easier suddenly become things that weigh us down, burden and worry us, things that need tending and taking care of, so much baggage to be carried around and shoved into some compartment over our heads. And then is when we hear God whisper, in the kindest possible voice, *You fool.*

Now we're connected with the writers of Ecclesiastes and Colossians and Luke, asking, *What is it that's lasting, that really matters in a world where we all go down to the grave?* And now we've finally gotten the point of all three lessons. We're finally asking the right questions. What is it that matters?

Alistair Cooke answered that question years ago in one of my favorite quotes. He said:

> *In the best of times our days are numbered anyway, and so it would be a crime against nature for any generation to take the world crisis so solemnly that it put off enjoying those things for which we were presumably designed in the first place ... the opportunity to do good work, to fall in love, to enjoy friends, to hit a ball, and to bounce a baby.*

I want to suggest this morning that these lessons are all about risk, about daring to make our lives something other than our culture teaches and expects. The challenge of these lessons is to set our own priorities in the light of our Christian faith. Our Christian faith is about more than a set of beliefs and a good worship experience on Sunday. If it's about anything, it's about a relationship with God that drastically changes our perception and appreciation of life. It's about a relationship that reorders our priorities, that makes the journey through life a risky adventure, sometimes a series of demanding and unpopular choices, and a mysterious love affair with the Creator and Sustainer of it all.

The task of our lives is to remember the lessons of our turbulent times and to *grow something besides old*. And there is a challenge here for us this morning. The challenge is to make our own list of priorities, as Alistair Cooke did. I want to challenge all of us today to write down in pen and ink a list of our life values. At the top of the list, let's write "a closer relationship with the Lord of my life." Then go on to put down our own announcements of what is important on this flight through time. And post it on the bathroom mirror or the refrigerator or wherever and read it every day. And dare to ask, each day, "Does my life match my list?"

We must risk asking if our lives witness to the life-changing presence of God and call ourselves back when our lives and our list disagree. Then, when our soul is demanded of us, we can know that it wasn't all vanity and chasing after wind but a life lived "in the name of the Lord Jesus, giving thanks to God the Father through him."   *Amen.*

Sunday Morning Dynamite

Season of Pentecost – Patricia R. Davis

So Jesus said to them, "Very truly, I tell you, unless you eat the flesh of the Son of Man and drink his blood, you have no life in you." John 6:53

She had always liked it when we brought communion to her bedside before. She seemed to recognize our white albs and she seemed to find comfort and a certain peace in receiving the Eucharist. But this time was entirely different. We entered her room, bearing the holy gifts, and announced that we were there to bring her communion. The words fairly exploded out of her mouth: "Get out! I don't want it! Get out! Get out!" The room was filled with panic and fear, an explosion of emotion in a small and intimate space. We left quickly ... but I wondered if her response isn't the one we should all feel: that this holy communion is a scary and dangerous thing, threatening to blow up our lives and destroy the comfort we've come to expect.

Annie Dillard said it in her book, *Teaching a Stone to Talk*:

On the whole, I do not find Christians, outside of the catacombs, sufficiently sensible of conditions. Does anyone have the foggiest idea what sort of power we so blithely invoke? Or as I suspect, does no one believe a word of it? The churches are [like] children playing on the floor with their chemistry sets, mixing up a batch of TNT to kill a Sunday morning. It is madness to wear ladies' straw hats and velvet hats to church; we should all be wearing crash helmets. Ushers should issue life preservers and signal flares; they should lash us to our pews.

What we do in church is powerful stuff. And there's plenty to be afraid of, plenty to upset our lives, plenty to offend everyone in today's lessons. It's time to put on our crash helmets and prepare to be assaulted by the word of the Lord. For this day, the reading from the Hebrew scriptures is taken from Joshua 24: 1-2a, 14-25. Joshua became a leader of the Israelites after Moses, but he got there by wading through the blood of conquered people, all supposedly under the approving gaze of God. And the threat is there for the Israelites, too. "If you forsake the Lord ... then he will turn and do you harm, and consume you ..." If this is the God that we worship, then we're going to have to rethink who he is and what he's about.

Then we come to Paul's letter to the Ephesians. It's a hard one for us to read with a straight face: "Wives, be subject to your husbands ... the husband is the head of the wife ..." The suggestion is also there that a woman is unclean and can only be made clean by the action of her husband. It was certainly an explosive letter, though for different reasons than it is today. In Paul's time, women were considered property, to be cared for or disposed of as cavalierly as a cow or slave or piece of land. A woman could be divorced for failing to produce a son or for failing to keep a clean house. For any number of infractions she could be divorced and thus outcast from her parents, her extended family and neighbors. So when Paul challenged early believers to treat their wives with the same love that Christ had for the church, to love their wives as they do their own bodies, it was revolutionary, offensive, and threatened to blow up the whole community. It's a passage that should still make us sit uneasily in our pews.

Then we come to today's lesson from John. Jesus has just finished explaining that those who follow him must "eat the flesh of the Son of Man and drink his blood." Now John was writing to a people familiar with Greek philosophy who would have understood the call to join Jesus in dying. But imagine hearing Jesus say *this* for the first time. First he says that he is the bread that came down from heaven, and everyone knows this is really just the son of Joseph and Mary, the boy from down the street. Then he says that, in spite of centuries of Jewish law forbidding contact with blood, in spite of that, they must consume his flesh and blood to have eternal life. Even if it's just a metaphor, it's ugly, gory and offensive. And the response of those who heard him is understandable: "This teaching is difficult; who can accept it?" That's very politely put. It probably felt more like the old woman all over again, "I don't want any! Get out!" But Jesus won't let up. He pushes them even farther! "Does this offend you? Then what if you were to see the Son of Man ascending to where he was before?" In other words, *what if I leave you right here and now and soar away on a cloud to heaven, leaving you to fend for yourselves?* It was an explosion in their midst and many ran away in fear and disgust. It was offensive and outrageous and too difficult to accept.

Perhaps that's the reason these passages are included in our lectionary. Because it's easy to follow Christ when what we're hearing are comfortable words, when Jesus seems to promise safety and healing for all that troubles us. But we hear the difficult passages and rush to equivocate, anxious to explain away what is offensive and disruptive. We can easily justify it: *It was written for a different time and a different people, Jesus was just speaking metaphorically, Jesus didn't really mean what he said, the Gospel writers didn't give us the whole story, or our translations are flawed.* There are lots of ways to avoid the havoc that a Gospel explosion will wreak on our lives.

The challenge of Jesus, though, is straightforward and demanding. "Does this offend you?" he asks. "How about when you go to work and find someone is after your job?" Our response, he says, must be an earth-shattering one. *Refuse to seek vengeance, refuse to return evil for evil, but turn the other cheek, go the extra mile, treat your co-worker with kindness, respect and compassion.* "How about when your son asks for his college fund and then blows it all on cars and girls and drugs?" Our response must be the explosive one, the unexpected one. *Love that child, love him though it hurts and he has rejected you and all that you would do for him, love him and never give up looking for him to come home.* Jesus asks us to live so that the explosions which occur in our lives don't destroy the world but instead, clear away the rubble and create a space for new life to grow.

Jesus talked of himself as the bread that has come down from heaven. It isn't bread that sits easily on the stomach. Sometimes everything in us wants to scream, "Get out! I don't want it!" Because it's often bread that promises real heartburn, as God seeks to burn away all that clutters our lives. It's bread that we eat, when we can bear to think of it, with fear and trembling, knowing that it will disrupt our lives and bring us to a different kind of chaos. It's bread leavened with dynamite, baked in the oven of everyday life and offered from the table of the One who knows the taste of it personally. And that may be the only reason we have the courage to eat this bread: because He has tasted it before us and found it to be very good. "To whom can we go?" There is only one answer. We go to the One who promises to reshape the landscape of our lives with a single bite of bread. We go to the Holy One of God, who has the words of eternal life. *Amen.*

The Peace of Christ

Season of Pentecost – John J. Capellaro

"Do you think that I have come to bring peace? ... No, I tell you, but rather division!" Luke 12:51

Saul stands by in awe – struck still over the insolence of this Stephen, this Jesus believer. "They all deserve to die, beginning with this one," he reasons. Centuries of tradition can be suddenly bent to fit the teachings of this so-called prophet? Belief in this Jesus is absurd in light of the sacred scriptures. Their beliefs are dangerous to our whole Jewish faith. It must stop."

As the crowd listening to Stephen grows, a light rain begins to fall. A stranger leans over to Saul and says, "This Stephen says that his Jesus of Nazareth will change the customs that Moses handed on to us!" Saul feels himself stiffening with rage. The murmurs grow into shouts, and then someone, he can't see who, picks up a rock and throws it at Stephen, hitting him in the ribs. Stephen keeps delivering his speech – with a nearly imperceptible wince. Another rock lands on the side of his face, and a trickle of blood drips from a cut. Quickly another rock, and another. All the while Stephen continues to speak. Finally Stephen's speech is drowned out by the shouts of the crowd and he drops to the ground under a deluge of stones. Suddenly all becomes quiet, and all that can be heard is the rain hitting the ground, with a soft hint of thunder in the distance. "The stoning is justified," Saul says under his breath as if to convince himself.

As Stephen lies in the mud, his thoughts swirl and he recalls the words of the one he now calls "Lord."

"Do you think that I have come to bring peace? ... No, I tell you, but rather division!"

These strange words now reassure Stephen, and he knows they will become a banner of encouragement for his community of believers. The rocks have stopped, but it is too late. Stephen has received his Baptism of stones. The death and new life that he has lived for – has begun. For the first time in his life, he is clear about where he belongs and to whom he belongs. In his final moment he *"...kneels down and cries out in a loud voice, 'Lord, do not hold this sin against them.' When he said this, he died."* (Acts 7:60) *"And Saul approved of their killing him."* (Acts 8:1)

In January of 1981, the pastor of Saint Paul Community Baptist Church in Flatbush Brooklyn called together twenty local pastors and the Borough President of Brooklyn at the time, Harrison Golden. The purpose of the meeting was to explore possibilities for improving the quality of life in this dangerous section of New York. When confronted by Pastor Youngblood to share his vision for Brooklyn, Borough President Golden appeared confused and replied, "Vision? What do you mean vision?" Reverend Youngblood gently coaxed him, "How do you see the future of Brooklyn?" Golden turned to his Deputy Borough President who was acting as sort of a racial interpreter for the day. "What is this? Vision? Is this some religious thing?" He had no answers, so Golden again faced Youngblood. "We have plans for the waterfront," the borough president offered. "We don't live on the waterfront," Reverend Youngblood cut in. "What's your vision for us?" "You want to talk about services?" Golden asked, reverting to his political reflexes. "You want some garbage cans?" "No," Reverend Youngblood said firmly. "We want to know what your vision is. Because we're going to be here for a long time." Golden's patience expired. "I don't have a vision," he snapped. "Then thank you very much for coming today," Youngblood replied. "That's it?" Golden asked. "Yes." Still baffled, Golden remained seated, as all twenty ministers stood up and left the room.[1]

That meeting, although ripe with division, empowered those twenty pastors and their congregations. From that day, they realized they were a part of something bigger than themselves – and they began to work together for change in ways that some never thought possible. The first

---

[1] Samuel G. Freedman, *Upon This Rock* (New York: HarperPerennial, 1994), 323-324.

project they took on was to challenge ten local storeowners who were short-weighing produce, overpricing, selling spoiled goods, and treating people abusively. On several consecutive Saturdays, scores of church-goers descended on the ten stores armed with clipboards and survey forms. Each wore a badge identifying themselves as an "Inspector." Each one filled their carts with moldy fruit, sour milk, and rusty cans, making notes about rat droppings behind refrigerators and week old meat on shelves. One storeowner looking at the curious gathering barked, "Get out of here or I'll call the police." The inspector replied, "Don't worry, we already did." Before leaving each store, the owners were presented with a list of violations and a contract to correct them. For those who declined to sign, a boycott was threatened. Within a few weeks, all but three owners agreed to the terms. Those remaining there were put out of business for their violations. The community of Saint Paul has moved from food stores to other winnable issues, getting three thousand missing street signs replaced, getting several vacant buildings demolished, and converting local brothels and drug dens into day care facilities and medical centers. None of this was accomplished without conflict and division. None of it.

"Do you think that I have come to bring peace? ... No, I tell you, but rather division!"

I had the chance to worship at Saint Paul Community Baptist Church two years ago, while visiting in New York. As we entered the church that Sunday morning and took our seats – we were treated to an hour of warm up music, led by over two hundred teenagers. Pastor Youngblood finally arrived, and greeted his congregation the way he does every Sunday: "This is a party, y'all." As the music answered him, a rhythm began to envelop the congregation that was contagious. Reverend Youngblood pounded the beat into the air fist after fist, like a fighter working the heavy bag ..."[2] and then began his preaching with the words from today's gospel.

"Do you think that I have come to bring peace? ... No, I tell you, but rather division!"

---

[2] Freedman, *Upon This Rock*, 3.

"Now we know about division – don't we?" And a murmur of uh-huhs and laughter filled the church. "And we know about division, because we are disciples of Jesus Christ." And a thousand AMENS shook the building.

Whenever the church is behaving like the church, there is always conflict with the values of the world, and therefore division. Whenever we are faced with choosing Christ or not choosing Christ – there will be conflict and division. I don't think it's too much to say that any faith community that is not in the midst of some conflict and division – rooted in a clash between the values of the world with the values of God's Kingdom – can't really be called a community of faith. And although it's hard work to live in that kind of tension, it is also exhilarating, especially when we know that we are in it together.

You may remember that Archbishop Njojo of the Congo paid us a visit last year in order to help raise awareness of the ongoing political and economic crises there, which has claimed millions of lives. The Virginia Pilot covered his visit with a very nice article. A few days after the article ran I received a letter accusing the people of St. Paul's – and me – of creating problems in race relations – that we were behaving like ignorant liberals in our support of Africans, who were nothing better than subhuman animals. It goes without saying, that the letter was unsigned.

"Do you think that I have come to bring peace? ... No, I tell you, but rather division!"

We are part of something bigger than any of us, and it is exhilarating to be among people of good faith, who have the courage to invite division and conflict by the example of their lives. It brings meaning to know that we are locked arm in arm helping one another stand in Christ's Light – opposed to those values of the world which breed superiority, selfishness, and fear. I pray that we remain embraced "... on a collision course with society ...,"[3] so that we may with one voice, joyfully proclaim:

"Do you think that Jesus has come to bring peace? ... No, I tell you, but rather division!"   Amen.

---

[3] Freedman, *Upon This Rock*, 37.

All Day Long

Season of Pentecost – Patricia R. Davis

Who will separate us from the love of Christ? Will hardship, or distress, or persecution, or famine, or nakedness, or peril, or sword? As it is written, "For your sake we are being killed all day long; we are accounted as sheep to be slaughtered." No, in all these things we are more than conquerors through him who loved us. Romans 8:35-36

When it was evening, the disciples came to him and said, "This is a deserted place, and the hour is now late; send the crowds away so that they may go into the villages and buy food for themselves." Jesus said to them, "They need not go away; you give them something to eat." Matthew 14:15-16

I have the day off and that by itself is enough to make it a wonderful day, even if I do have errands to run. First, off to the gas station to fill up the car. I'm standing there with the pump in hand when a woman pulls up next to me, three small children in the back seat. I can hear her yelling through the closed windows before she ever gets out of her car. To say she has reached the end of her rope is an understatement. The children cower in the back seat, crying, and I feel like crying too.

For your sake we are being killed all day long ...

I pull out of the gas station and head down the road toward the grocery store. But I must have done something wrong because a man in a blue car zooms around me, horn blaring, his hand raised in that universal gesture of disrespect. What started out as a great day is rapidly becoming a test of endurance, little pieces of me dying every few minutes it seems.

For your sake we are being killed all day long ...

Grocery shopping done, I'm writing out a check for our family's food as the cashier loads my things into bags. She doesn't look at me. I ask her, "May I have my change in ones, please?" When she doesn't answer, I figure she hasn't heard me and I repeat myself, "May I have my change in ones, please?" "I heard you and I'm getting it," she snarls. And little pieces of my spirit give up the ghost.

For your sake we are being killed all day long ...

When Paul quoted this line from Psalm 44 in his letter to the church in Rome, he was speaking of a threat much more personal and much more lethal. He *was* in danger of being killed. But it rings true for us today, that sense of being killed *all day long*, so that we come rushing in here on a Sunday morning, praying, please God, for an hour of peace, just a few moments of being fed instead of having bites taken out of us.

Jesus might have said the same thing when faced with the hungry masses sitting on the hillside. It had been a day unlike any other. It began with the news of John's death; John, the Baptizer, John, his cousin, mentor and friend, killed by a dark power shadowing the horizon. So Jesus, bearing his grief, wanted only to get away. Into a boat, on the sea, maybe the warm water would wash away his sadness and fear in another sort of baptism. But it wasn't to be. The people followed, more and more of them, until, when he came ashore, there was nothing left to do but tell them all to sit down and to summon from some unexplainable depth, yet more of himself to give away. They were so hungry for him. Everyone wanted a piece of him.

And the disciples were no better. They might as well have been just part of the crowd, for all the help they were to Jesus. Just more hungry mouths to feed, twelve more people wanting a piece of him, part of the problem rather than part of the solution.

And this is what I thought of when I put side by side those episodes from my day off and these lessons about feeding and being fed. Because I thought that if we come here only seeking to be fed and don't go out of here with enough left over, not only to sustain us, but to feed the hungry people out there, then the rest of the week we will feel as though we are being killed all day long.

Last week John Capellaro quoted Archbishop Rowan Williams in a stunning bit of insight. Listen to it again:

> *If I see the world as related to God before it is related to me, or if I see another person as related to God before he or she is related to me, then my approach to the world or that other person is different. It's not my possession; he or she is not someone for me to master, persuade, teach, or devour. They are somebody else's first ...*

They are somebody else's first. They belong to Christ; they are part of that tired, cranky, irritable, complaining, hungry crowd needing to be fed. And if I can see them as Christ's own, then I can obey Christ when everything in me tells me nothing will do any good; there isn't enough in all the world to feed their need.

I worry sometimes that we have taken the fierce independence that was so necessary for starting this country of ours and translated it into a fierce personal creed that says, "Justice for all means justice for me first." And it doesn't seem to be working very well at all. We are living as people "being killed all day long" instead of as people who know that nothing "will be able to separate us from the love of God in Christ Jesus." We are living, not as "more than conquerors" because of this love, but as people who must conquer others or feel defeated. We've become a people ready to take offense and ready to defend ourselves. So when we're cut off in traffic, we fight back with our own brand of justice to prove that we won't be treated unjustly. We give rude gestures too and honk our horn and get angry at the idiots who would spoil our day. And when we're spoken to rudely in the store, we respond in kind, leaving in the checkout lane a few more people, wounded and dying. Or when we see a desperate mother taking it out on her children, we conduct an inner dialogue about how useless and terrible she is and dismiss her as certainly not one of Christ's own.

But what if all these people, what if everyone who does anything unkind or rude or just plain mean, is simply someone who's hungry? That angry driver, a man hungry for something to make him feel special and valuable. That screaming mother, hungry to feel that she's more than a slave to everyone else's needs. That tired cashier, hungry for more meaning in her life. What if we were to see their behavior as a symptom of an anxious, gnawing inner hunger? Then, we might just hear Jesus saying, "These, too, belong to me. You give them something to eat."

Imagine. A day in which every unkindness was met with food: food for the body maybe, food for the soul surely. A day in which that informal Eucharist on the hillside is repeated again and again, in the grocery store, on the highway, at the gas station. It might be that Eucharist in those places would sound like the whisper of a prayer for the man in the blue car, a blessing on someone roaring away from his hunger for God. It might be that Eucharist would sound like a word of encouragement for the hard job of mothering. It might be that the Eucharist would look like an unexpected smile and some help bagging the groceries to an irritable cashier.

A Eucharist, bread and fish in disguise, passed around to all sorts of people whose hunger makes them tired and cranky, irritable and desperate. We can celebrate this Eucharist all day long, in all kinds of strange and wonderful ways because we've seen where it comes from. And we know that, by the grace of God, there is more than enough, loaves and fishes for everyone. If we are being killed all day long, let's make sure it's for Christ's sake. And give them something to eat. *Amen (Let it be so).*

Heaven-Hungry Hearts

Season of Pentecost – Patricia R. Davis

Someone asked Jesus, "Lord, will only a few be saved?" He said to them, "Strive to enter through the narrow door; for many, I tell you, will try to enter and not be able." Luke 13: 23-24

There's an old, slightly tacky joke about our ideas of heaven and who will be there; it illustrates some of that strange theological thinking that we can get so wrapped up in.

It seems a woman died and went to heaven where she was met by St. Peter, who offered to show her around before she got settled in. As they were taking the tour, they came upon a group of people gathered around tables intently studying some cards in front of them. Every once in a while, someone would wave excitedly and yell, *Bingo! As you may have guessed,* said St. Peter, *those are the Catholics.* They went a little farther on, and saw a group of very well dressed ladies sitting at linen covered tables, eating exquisite desserts and drinking tea from bone china cups. *Who are they?* asked the woman, and St. Peter answered, *Why those are the Episcopalians, of course.* Finally they came to a large area completely enclosed by a heavy maroon velvet curtain. From within the curtain the woman could hear the murmur of hundreds of voices. *What's going on in there,* she asked. *Shhh,* said St. Peter, *those are the Baptists and they think they're the only ones here!*

This silly story addresses some of the questions and problems raised by today's Gospel lesson. The first of these problems is with the word "strive," which suggests that we have to do something to earn our way into heaven, to "work out our own salvation with fear and trembling", as Paul would say to the Philippians. It's a seductive idea in our

179

achievement-oriented culture, but it isn't a new one. And there's the related question of just who will enjoy the fruits of the kingdom, with the suggestion that Jesus will refuse to recognize people who have been spending lots of time with him all along. It's all wrapped up in a confused collection of phrases and ideas that sound unlike the good news we're used to hearing from Jesus.

One key lies in the very first line, in which we learn that Jesus is traveling toward Jerusalem. He's journeying toward death and the pressure is on; every moment, every encounter, matters because each will be his last. He wants us to know that something of life-saving proportions is happening and we mustn't miss it. There can't be any more half-hearted hanging around because we haven't anything better to do. This striving that he's talking about isn't about working out our own salvation; that is done for us. It is about getting focused, about knowing what's important and refusing to be distracted.

So if we want to be in on an amazing transformation, Jesus tells us, we're going to have to do more than be from the same town or the same church or the same social group. We're going to have to get up close and personal and lay ourselves open to the fact that God may have some transforming work to do in us too. We're going to have to strive to remain focused on the most important thing in any and every life – our relationship with the Lord of that life. It just might be that while everyone is invited to the dinner party, we do have to RSVP – with our very selves.

So if the emphasis is on our own response, it should make short work of the second problem posed in this passage, the problem of who else will be there. All of our obsessions with other people's behavior, all of our not-so-subtle distinctions between who's in and who's out, who qualifies for credit as good Christians and who's just going through the motions, are simply examples of losing focus, of reneging on the invitation. Jesus tells us in his parable that we can't know and we're wasting our time trying. The people in the kingdom of God are going to be a strange conglomeration, with some real surprises on both sides of the door. (That's just in case we think you have to be Catholic or Episcopalian or Baptist – or Christian!) The kingdom of God is going to be a surprise all around. In fact, if we're paying attention, we can see it already happening, odd collections of people going through the door.

For example: a nurse asked me to visit Mrs. Brown last week. *She's dying and her family is in there*, she said. *I think they could use your company.* So I went in.

She lay there, a large woman spread out over the bed like her own down comforter, her hands lying open and still on the sheets. She was breathing the breath of the dying, a sort of gasping that seems like work, but there was no strain on her face, no tightening of the shoulders or furrowing of the brow to tell us there was any pain. She lay still and quiet, her eyes closed to this world, only occasionally opening as though hoping for a glimpse of the next.

Around her bed sat four women keeping watch, four ties to this life, daughter, cousin, niece and friend. But this was no passive sitting and waiting. These women were dressed! Dressed in Sunday finery, dressed to the nines and made up and perfumed – "angels in festal gathering" – this was a vigil that they were determined to keep in style! There would be no haphazard, casual send-off for Mrs. Brown. They were there to see her through with the best that they had to offer.

These four women sat around her bed, enclosing her within an invisible but palpable wall of love, their devotion forming a boundary of protection. And I walked into the middle of this sacred vigil. It's the most awkward time in any pastoral visit, those first few minutes when I dare to break in on a family united by profound emotion and presume to offer something. We talked quietly, about her breathing, her illness, who was related to whom, and about how this time felt heavy and a little fearsome. They were a tightly bound family and that wall stood solid and impenetrable as I, I stood at the end of the bed and hoped to understand how I might be helpful.

But there wasn't anything to do, anything to fix it and make it all better … I asked if we might have prayer together … and suddenly, there was a door in the wall. These elegant women unhooked the latch and threw it open and let me in, into their grief and into their company. We laid our hands all over the dying woman, and I began to pray. And as I began to speak, something in that room changed. In good Baptist fashion, the women joined in as I prayed, their voices echoing and re-echoing. *Lord, we ask your blessing*, I said, and I heard, *Your blessing,*

Lord, your blessing ... comfort her ... oh, Jesus ... touch her ... take away our fear ... hold her in your arms ... fill us with your love ... five voices now joined in prayer and praise, the words floating over and around our heads like so many soap bubbles blown from a child's bubble wand. The door was open, open between this world and the next, and we went in.

Then I anointed Mrs. Brown with oil – oil from the stock you at St. Paul's have given me for just such ministry, and the door opened wider, this time into their own lives. *Please, would you anoint me? I have terrible arthritis. I have high cholesterol. I'm worried about my son. I've had a stroke.* Prayer and anointing and heartfelt hugs all around and that room was transformed into the kingdom of God and I was so glad to be there. Because the kingdom of God is wherever people open the narrow door of their own hearts and allow another to enter in. It comes when the walls of our lives are opened to the possibility of transformation, not just in that future life, but today.

We can't figure out how it happens or how it will happen, and if we're trying to do so, we're putting all our striving toward the wrong thing. Because striving for the narrow door is about "cultivating heaven-hungry hearts" with anyone and everyone who shows up, and being first or last or somewhere in the middle is *all* good news. It's about the future kingdom, of course, but even more, it's about the kingdom here and now – a transformation we don't have to wait until death to experience. Jesus is about getting everyone in the kingdom and he means to start now with all those people from north and south and east and west who have heard that something wonderful is happening and whose heaven-hungry hearts won't let them rest until they are fed. *Amen.*

I Wanna Be in the Club!

Season of Pentecost – John J. Capellaro

... the Pharisees and the scribes asked him, "Why do your disciples not live according to the tradition of the elders, but eat with defiled hands?" Jesus said to them, "Isaiah prophesied rightly about you hypocrites, as it is written, 'This people honors me with their lips, but their hearts are far from me; in vain do they worship me, teaching human precepts as doctrines.' You abandon the commandment of God and hold to human tradition." Mark 7:5-8

It must be that "Belonging" is the most important thing in the world. It seems the clearer we are about our belonging, the more secure we are. It's a bit of what we're hearing in Mark's gospel today. We're overhearing one of those 1st century debates where both Jewish and non-Jewish disciples of Jesus are trying to figure out what it takes to be in the same community with each other. Who really belongs and who doesn't? The gospel offers a story in which Jesus calls into question one of those standards of belonging: Jewish Purity Laws. As Jesus ministers to both Jew and non-Jew, he asks those who challenge him, "Who cares whether my disciples wash their hands before eating? Is that what it takes to belong? If it's filth you're worried about – look within yourself." This has to be one of Jesus' favorite teachings. "Stop wagging your fingers at others – and instead look inside yourselves to see what is unclean. Look for what hinders *Your Own Belonging* – to God."

When I was in 9th grade, like most insecure teenagers, I was utterly preoccupied with belonging. The rules for belonging were very clear. There were particular clothing items, hairstyles, and even language rules that applied. *("Cool man," which over the next decade would evolve all the way to "Far Out, man!")* A few of us decided to form a rock n' roll band, which allowed us to really "belong." It was 1965 and we called ourselves, *The Barons*. We played "Hang on Sloopy," "Louie, Louie," "Wipeout," and a very white version of "Midnight Hour." We were horrible. We even had uniforms. We wore cuffed chinos, buckskin shoes, blue oxford button down shirts, navy silk knit ties, and 3-button India Madras sportcoats. God, did we belong! Towards the end of the school year, we were asked to play a sweet 16 party at *The Club*. Now having grown up in a blue collar town and only recently made my way into a nicer neighborhood, my family never belonged to *The Club* – so this was a special treat for me. It was a club in suburban Philadelphia and it was posh. We were even going to be paid. We got the job because three of our band member's families were members of *The Club*, and our guitarists' dad was on the Board of *The Club*. He *really* belonged.

Well, I was so excited about the job, I invited my best friend to come along. His name was Ira Silverstein. When Ira arrived, the other guys in the band started to act funny. Now they knew Ira, and they knew he was my best friend, so I couldn't understand why they were acting weird. A few minutes later our guitarist's dad showed up – the one who was on the Board. He approached Ira and me and politely explained that this was a private club and a private party, and that Ira would have to leave, which he did. I learned the following week that *The Club* didn't allow Jews in, and that even the presence of this young Jewish boy was uncomfortable for the membership. I never realized that grownups were just as insecure as teenagers and made up such strange rules for belonging. I never went back to *The Club*.

It *is* our insecurities that make us behave this way. A secure person would never make rules to exclude people. A secure community wouldn't waste their time worrying about how to keep others out. I'm glad God is secure. That's why God doesn't put up hurdles. That's why Jesus' message of inclusion is so godlike. I guess that's why so many people believe that Jesus is the reflection of God. I guess that's why Jesus spent most of his time hanging out with folks who don't belong. Maybe that's why it's the broken people – the people who don't fit in – who seem to know Jesus best. Maybe that's why *we* know Jesus best when we are most broken. There are no rules for "belonging" with Jesus

– except to know our brokenness.   Church is supposed to be the community where we *can* admit that – where we can let go of all the silly, insecure rules for belonging that infect the rest of our lives.   And yet church is often the worst of all in setting barriers for belonging.   How many churches set all kinds of hurdles to clear before you can join.   Thank God there are some churches that don't.   I'm glad the Ethiopian eunuch got baptized after a brief chariot ride with Phillip, and a story or two about Jesus.   "As they were going along the road, they came to some water; and the eunuch said, 'Look, here is water!   What is to prevent me from being baptized?'   And Phillip said, 'Nothing my friend.' "   Nothing – not yet anyway.'   But just wait – the Church will find something.

How often we drag people through our own silly little rituals – to belong!   "You can't run for vestry until you've been a parishioner for how long?   You can't vote at the annual church meeting until you've had some letter transferred."   Most people joining the Episcopal Church today are not coming from another Episcopal church.   Most newer members here don't know what "letters" are – thank God!   There is very little denominational loyalty anymore.   People are finally beginning to act on their hunch that Methodist, Episcopal, Catholic, Presbyterian, and Lutheran are labels that are not essential to faith.   Our differences have begun to dissolve.   I suspect that's the work of the Holy Spirit – tearing down the walls of separation – eliminating barriers to belonging – *"leveling the mountains and raising up the valleys, "* I think is how Isaiah put it.

The fact is we do belong to something far more significant than our little clubs, far more significant than church, even far more significant than our families.   We belong to the source of all life and love, by God's gracious gift, and there is nothing we can do to alter that.   We gather here to celebrate that fact.   We pray, dear God, that we may never tell someone what they have to do to belong – but rather show them that they *do* belong.   We pray that we may never politely explain how many years it takes to belong, but rather that we may act as if we actually believe the teachings of Jesus – for their sake – for our sake – for Christ's sake.   *Amen.*

Take a Child to Work Day

Season of Pentecost – Patricia R. Davis

A man had two sons; he went to the first and said, "Son, go and work in the vineyard today." He answered, "I will not"; but later he changed his mind and went. Matthew 21: 28-29

Jesus must have been a most interesting teenager! At any rate, he certainly seems to have remembered what it was like because in the gospels we hear all sorts of stories about teenagers. The story of the prodigal son is a famous one: two boys who, from their descriptions, just have to be teenagers: one the dutiful, obedient but resentful older brother and the other, a younger child, desperate to get away from his father's house, desperate to make his own way and to find out for himself what the world is like. Can't we remember what that felt like? And now we have today's story, another father with two sons, and you can tell they're teenagers. Their father comes in and says to both children, "Today is 'take your children to work day' and I'd really like you to come and see what I do all day" and one says, "Oh, sure, Dad, I'd love to come" but he never gets around to it. He's probably on the phone with his girlfriend and listening to his favorite CDs. The time gets away from him and he just never makes it. The other son says, "Aw, Dad, not today. I've got all this homework to do! And besides, you don't really need me." So the father goes off and it's the son who at first refused to go who turns up to help out. We've all seen this happen or been part of it. And this is just like Jesus, using the everyday events of our lives to tell us up-to-date stories about where and how God might be found.

This story is one of three readings for today with a common theme. In the lesson from Ezekiel (chapter 18:1-4, 25-32), God says that old

186

adage about the children paying the price for their father's sins doesn't apply any longer. God says everyone belongs to him and he doesn't take pleasure in anyone falling short of the life he has in mind for us. In the lesson from Phillipians (2:1-13), Paul says, *Complete my joy by being of the same mind, having the same love*, that love coming from a life lived in friendship with Jesus. And in the Gospel lesson, Jesus says the tax collectors and prostitutes have a special place in God's heart because no one is left out based on the externals... it's what happens on the inside that matters to God. These lessons are about a call to repentance for sure, but it's a call with a twist. It's not just that God calls us to obedience but that God calls us to be his children now, to live as he has designed us in this world! God wants to share the wonder of life lived in companionship with him, and God's creative love promises so much more than we could possibly dream of.

So I was thinking about the two sons in the Gospel story and what happened on that day when their father asked them to come to work with him. Both of these young people heard their father's voice, but they had different responses. The one son sounded like he would be glad to help but he just never quite made it. He probably had a good day anyway. But, he didn't spend the day with his father. He didn't get to see his father working to take care of him, didn't get to see what it cost his father to keep him fed and cared for, didn't get to see how the world looks through his father's eyes. He didn't have the pleasure of finding out more about this person who gave him his life. The other son, to be sure, wasn't any too anxious to spend the day doing something he hadn't planned on, but he went anyway. Maybe it was guilt, or duty, or any of the dozens of reasons that we do what we don't really want to do, but I bet he was surprised at what he saw and learned about his father that day.

The commentaries will say that all of these readings are talking about repentance, which is one of those words we avoid a lot. It carries such connotations of sin, of gloom and doom, of being found wanting and being punished. But, in truth, to repent means simply "to turn." It's to turn from what we've been doing and to do something new. It may well mean dealing with some sin that is weighing us down but the idea is that we are then freed to be something more.

Repentance – to turn. Such a turn can be as earthshaking as Paul's conversion on the road to Damascus or, as Jesus suggests, as common as going to work with your father. It can be as simple as refusing to come back with the sarcastic response when we're angry. Or it can be as dramatic as turning away from a high-powered New York career to become a priest, for God's sake, with a different kind of power, rooted in love. It can happen on an ordinary day when we have something else in mind entirely. The simplest times in our lives can be occasions for God to show us something new, about ourselves and about Him.

It was just such a day that led me to become a nursing home chaplain. I had been visiting this particular nursing home for some time because we had a parishioner there and I thought that maybe this was a place that could use my time as a volunteer. But when I went in to spend a whole day visiting people, instead of just a few minutes, it was awful. First of all, it was kind of dark and smelly. And there were so many people who seemed in such terrible shape. And it was positively draining to listen to their troubles and to care and not be able to do anything concrete to help. So when I got ready to leave after my first full day there, I was more than ready! I couldn't wait to get out of there! I was on my way down the hall, all the while telling God that this just wasn't for me; I don't have what it takes to do this. Anyway, going down the hall on my way out, I happened to glance in one of the rooms. In the bed was a very old woman. Her white hair was fanned out in a messy spray on the pillow and she was stretching out one long, painfully thin arm toward a cup of water on the bedside table, just out of reach. Well, I thought, I can at least help with that, and I turned and went in. I held the cup for her as she drank greedily from the straw and then she laid her head on the pillow and said, "I was so thirsty." And in that moment, I heard the voice of Jesus, begging a drink of water from the woman at the well.

A turning … a place where God beckons us to leave the narrow hallways of our lives and enter new rooms, rooms where he is waiting to be found, where we can be part of his work of redeeming the world. This God, who has formed us in the womb, who knew us before we were born, wants us to come along as He goes about his work! So God calls us and beckons us and we are afraid, as though it will mess up our lives, destroy all of our carefully made plans. It may! And we can choose to avoid going out with him. We can even have pretty good lives without ever really committing ourselves to God's call to us as his children. But we will miss so much! We will miss a life lived as his honest-to-God children. As we read in 1 John 3, *See what love the Father has given us, that we should be called children of God; and that is what we are ... Beloved, we are God's children now; what we will be has not yet been revealed.*

I dare say, both of the sons in today's story loved their father and were loved by him, but only one of them found out what it was like to spend the day with him, to really be with someone who loves you more than his own life. This is the son who heeded the call to step out of his perfectly happy life and into LIFE! He is the one who discovered that working alongside God is not about earning salvation but about living out salvation. He discovered the truth of our powerful Morning Prayer that "we show forth thy praise, not only with our lips, but in our lives, by giving up our selves to thy service." The son who went found his deliverance "from the presumption of coming to this Table for solace only, and not for strength; for pardon only, and not for renewal." Strength, renewal, salvation, wholeness ... the promises of God who is at work in us, both to will and to work for his good pleasure.

An earthly father with two sons, a heavenly father with countless children – and in between the stories, a God who has in mind only that we should participate in His Spirit, have the same love, complete His joy, if we will only turn ... and live!

Mapping the Dead Zones

Season of Pentecost – Patricia R. Davis

Then Jesus told them a parable about the need to pray always and not to lose heart. He said, "In a certain city there was a judge who neither feared God nor had respect for people. In that city there was a widow who kept coming to him and saying, 'Grant me justice against my opponent.' For a while he refused; but later he said to himself, 'Though I have no fear of God and no respect for anyone, yet because this widow keeps bothering me, I will grant her justice, so that she may not wear me out by continually coming.' " And the Lord said, "Listen to what the unjust judge says. And will not God grant justice to his chosen ones who cry to him day and night? Will he delay long in helping them? I tell you, he will quickly grant justice to them."
Luke 18:1-8a

There was an article in the newspaper some months ago that so struck me that I've had it on the refrigerator ever since. It seems that scientists have mapped an area in the Gulf of Mexico where there is so little oxygen in the water that no marine life can survive. Covering more than 8000 square miles, this hypoxic body of water extends from the coast of Louisiana down to Texas and as far as 50 miles out to sea. It seems to be growing in size and is called a "dead zone" because nothing can live there. A "dead zone" ... where anything that ventures there finds emptiness and air-hunger and slow death. And I thought when I read this article, that we've all known people like that, people who suck the air right out of the room, people whose hearts have vast dead zones

190

where there should be life.

We meet one of them in the parable in today's Gospel. The story begins with an editorial comment that the parable is about the need to pray always. Good advice, but it's a comment that can narrow our vision and keep us from looking at the whole picture. Granted, the story is about the contrast between God's ready generosity and the judge's stinginess. But our attention gets stuck on this troubling judge, a man who should be ultimately concerned with justice and mercy but instead is only concerned with his own comfort. A man who isn't ashamed to admit that he has "no fear of God and no respect for anyone." An article in the newspaper about him might call him hard-nosed, strictly judicial, and unable to be swayed from a strictly legal interpretation. And after all, the law was clear. A widow had no right to inheritance and if a woman's husband died, well that was too bad. She would have to make the best of it. If her husband's family refused to take care of her, well, she probably deserved it. She must have done something to alienate them but, hey, sorry about that! This is a judge who lives and dies by the law, and who is already dead inside … a walking "dead zone."

This parable comes at an interesting place in the Gospel of Luke. It comes right after a lesson about Jesus' last days in which he says, *Whoever seeks to gain his life will lose it, but whoever loses his life will save it*. And this parable comes right before the lesson about the Pharisee and the tax collector who went up to pray. You remember the Pharisee who went to the temple and unselfconsciously catalogued his merits. His statements were all true, as were the judge's in this parable, but they both reveal a remarkable *self-satisfaction* … they both carry in their hearts a "dead zone" where nothing can really live.

As I said, we've all known people like this. But the danger with any story is that it becomes easy to let it be a story about someone else. We hear of a hard-hearted judge and we can name the people we know who are like that. If they would only ask, we could tell them exactly how deep and how wide are the dead zones in their hearts. And we know people who suck the air right out of a room, and we steer well clear of them. And all the time, we're walking around with our own dead zones. We, too, can have places inside us where nothing can live, where everything that enters is starved for light and air, and we can get only too comfortable with that.

So how does it happen that people who are born as beautiful, trusting infants, become adults with dead zones in their hearts, places where all that enters dies? We know some of the things that kill a human heart. Abuse – physical, verbal, sexual – can create a huge dead zone where nothing dares enter. A person can only stand so many assaults before the air goes out of her and the heart dies. Unremitting stress can create dead zones when every ounce of energy is used up just keeping the head above water. Disappointment after disappointment loaded on an unprepared heart can cause that heart to sink beneath the surface of despair and cynicism. And sometimes it's just a never-ending weariness that says, *This is all there is to life, and all there ever will be.* Our human hearts are susceptible to all kinds of dead zones.

My husband says this sermon should be called "Top Ten Ways You Know You Have a Dead Heart." So here goes. You know you have a dead heart when:

10. In any argument with your spouse, you know exactly what he/she is going to say.

9. You figure your job is just what you're doing until the real thing comes along.

8. You can tell exactly what kind of person someone is by the clothes they're wearing.

7. When asked for donations at the office, you say, *I give at church* and when asked for donations at church you say, *I give at the office.*

6. If your children turned out well, you take full credit for being a good parent. If they have lots of problems, it's their own darn fault; what's a parent to do?

5. If someone treats you unkindly, you cut them off. After all they need to know there are consequences to their behavior and you don't deserve to be treated like that.

4. You don't pray anymore because God knows what you need anyway and doesn't need to be bothered when he's as busy as you are.

3. You know the entire liturgy by heart and figure everyone else should too if they're going to be an Episcopalian.

2.   You think that all ministers should be as patient as Job, as articulate as St. Paul and as forgiving as Jesus.
1.   You secretly think that if everyone were more like you, the world would be a better place.

I'm trying to be funny here but, really, it's too easy. And before we know it, we have a whole assortment of dead spaces where nothing can live and grow. And if we're not careful, these dead zones blend together inside us until there is an ocean where the only justice is our justice and the only respect is the respect we think we're owed.

The challenge of this parable of the unjust judge is for us to map our own dead zones. We need to find the places where we've appointed ourselves the judge, the places where we have no fear of God and no respect for anyone. And then to summon up the courage and the humility to take on the role of the persistent widow. We must demand that God give us what we were created for – healing of those dead zones in our lives; in short, His own heart where our lifeless one lies. This is a prayer that can be prayed over and over, every day of our lives.

And the remarkable thing about all this is that Jesus died precisely for our persistent dead zones. He didn't give his life as a reward for our exemplary behavior. He came precisely for those of us who are drowning in our own dead zones, who can't keep our heads above water, who've never understood what it means to be really full of life. It is our deadness that cries out to God for resurrection. And it's that very death inside us that God wants to revive, to fill with light and teeming varieties of life.

There's one really good reason that Luke was so adamant that we should pray and keep on praying. It's because prayer is the way that we open ourselves to the oxygen-rich ocean of God's love. It's the life buoy that will save us from dead hearts and dead zones and dead lives. *Amen.*

It's So Nice Being Right!

Season of Pentecost – John J. Capellaro

*... God I thank you that I am not like other people: thieves,
rogues, adulterers, or even like this tax collector ...* Luke 18:11

The two of them stood in the hallway – squaring off with one
another again. One, the Psychologist in charge of the Children and
Youth unit of the mental hospital – the other a nine-year old boy,
named Nathan. The Psychologist was reprimanding Nathan for
violating another one of her rules that she kept adding to the already
long list. Nathan had shut down – again – and was frozen. I was there
to meet with the Psychologist to discuss a Bible Study that I was trying
to start with the kids on the unit. I approached them to ask if I could
help, and she quickly said, "No. I have things under control, thank
you." I looked at Nathan and asked if he was okay, and she answered for
him, "He's fine, thank you. We're just getting clear on the rules again."
She then added, "I guess you're here to find about that Bible study you
want to start with the children." "Yes, that's right," I answered. She
said, "Well, I've thought about it, and I suppose it's all right on two
conditions:

1.   You use the King James Version of the Bible, and
2.   You present an outline of your planned discussions with the
      children to me ahead of time."

I said that I just wanted to read them some Bible stories and ask the
kids what they made of them, and that I'd rather use a version of the
Bible they might actually understand. She insisted that The King James

194

was the only version of the bible that I could use because – to quote her precisely, "That's the one God wrote." When I tried to explain when and where the King James Bible came about, she stormed off down the hall, sweetly saying over her shoulder that the Bible study was not approved. I looked at Nathan, knelt down next to him, and said how sorry I was. Nathan looked at me and said, "It's okay, Chaplain John. Maybe God's punishing us, because I was bad."

Self-righteousness – especially religious self-righteousness is a hideous thing – whether it is expressed by well-meaning, misguided psychologists, fundamentalist Muslims determined to bring a narrow justice to their people and kill anyone who denies Allah, or overly-zealous Christians whose fervor for "right-belief" scares off thousands who want to gently explore whether or not Jesus can be found in today's church. Certitude about the divine mysteries of God is not faith. It's blind self-righteousness. Faith is to trust in that which we cannot know, and to live differently because of that trust. And yet, we are all self-righteous. We carry with us sets of certainties that we impose on one another, that tear down and infect. And yet, we are also humble sinners. Although perhaps more rare, we also carry within us that humility and the trust that God *is*, before whom we can only whisper, "'God, be merciful to me, a sinner!'" We are both that psychologist and nine-year old Nathan.

Last week we heard a story from Luke's gospel that helped us discover how we all have dead zones in our hearts and that persistent prayer can help us find life for those dead zones. We saw ourselves in each of the two characters from Luke's gospel – a cold-hearted judge and a persistent widow. In these two characters we were reminded that we all carry dead zones within us – *and* that we all carry within us the hope and potential of redemption through trust and prayer. And just in case there were some of us who thought we might be exempt from carrying those dead zones, Patti read off her top ten list of ways to know that our hearts are – at least in part – dead.

Well today we have a story that continues Luke's theme of discovering the broken and the hopeful within us all. We have two men who go to the Temple to pray. One offers his thanks that he's not like other people: "I live right; I follow the rules. Most others don't." The other man, standing far off, would not look up, and beating his breast says, *"God, be merciful to me, a sinner!"* The parable urges us to face and name the things we carry that keep us separated from God and one another, so that trust and relationship can be restored. The parable also coldly insists that if we pretend we have it all together – if our self-righteousness overrides our humility – there's not much God can do with us. Absolute certainty about anything is difficult to be around – but in areas of religion is insufferable. If these stories we have in the gospel really were told by Jesus, then I don't know what to expect in the next life. Jesus seems determined to unseat the religiously confident – the self-righteous – and to be God's agent for the outsider. If these stories really are of God, it wouldn't surprise me that the next life may greet the very certain with exact opposite of what they expect. Can you picture fundamentalist Muslims being greeted in the next life by a smiling Jesus, with white robe and beard, surrounded by the apostles, Mary, Joseph, and by all those killed in the name of Allah, with a gigantic rotating Cross behind them all, that has billions of light bulbs flashing on and off, "JESUS SAVES"? Of course, that's funny only if we can also imagine fundamentalist Christians arriving in the next life and being greeted by a Hindi-chanting Vishnu, surrounded by all those who have died at the hands of Christian slave-traders and Ku Klux Klanners.

The self-righteousness that Jesus' parables rail against has all kinds of expressions. Following Patti Davis' lead from last week, I've done my own top-ten list of things that can help us discover our self-righteousness. Ready?

You know that you are self-righteous when:

#10. You know the right way to do church and those other people don't!

#9. You feel sorry for all the people who have never experienced God, because they're not Christians.

#8. You are eager to reach out to others in need before you ask them if they want anything in the first place, or if they actually want it from *you!*

#7. Whatever accompanied your first experience of God, whether it was a certain style of music, church building, or prayer, is the thing you insist on recreating in order to experience God again – as if God won't reveal Himself to you unless those things are in place!

#6. You feel best about yourself when you look around and remember that just about everybody else is a loser!

#5 You get a real lift when you gaze at your new 240 HP SUV for about an hour!

#4. Your academic credentials, address, family lineage, geographical heritage, portfolio, salary, or title on your business card actually give you value.

#3. You don't bother to pray because God never delivered on that really important request.

#2. You find yourself starting any sentence with the words, "In my day …"   (If you're still with us, this *is* your day!)

And the number 1 way you can tell if you are self-righteous:

#1. If you've ever said anything even remotely close to this: "If only other people could know how nice it is to wear hand-made English shoes!"

The good news is this: We are all both humble sinners who know our shortcomings *and* blind, self-righteousness people. We stand before God together in all our humility and in all our brokenness. God's redemption is available to us equally. We receive what God offers us in Jesus Christ not because we are acknowledged sinners – not because we are self-righteous people in need of redemption – but rather in spite of those facts.

May we embrace our brokenness again today – may we celebrate the humility which survives in us all and God's very real presence among us – may we face the self-righteousness that lives in us all – and trembling ... may we whisper together, "God, be merciful to me, a sinner!" Amen.

Goliath Lives!

Season of Pentecost – John J. Capellaro

Jesus sat down, called the twelve, and said to them, "Whoever wants to be first must be last of all and servant of all." Then he took a little child and put it among them; and taking it in his arms, he said to them, "Whoever welcomes one such child in my name welcomes me, and whoever welcomes me welcomes not me but the one who sent me." Mark 9:35-37

There is a Goliath in our midst. There is a Goliath who tells us how to think and stifles our freedom, who blinds us with new cars, and drugs us with images of storybook lovers. This Goliath rapes the nobility out of life and displays what's left on prime time. This Goliath teases us with lottery tickets and ab machines and smothers us with visions of greatness. This Goliath is all that fuels our sense of security in the things of this world. It distracts us from that which is heroic and tricks us into using our creativity to serve self. It bends the minds of our political parties into thinking that winning matters more than serving the common good. This Goliath has many names and is the Wizard in many lands of Oz.

Goliath lives in the Stock Market and seduces us into thinking that return on investment matters more than the companies we invest in. Goliath vacations in Hollywood and shops on Rodeo Drive, where image always supersedes substance. Goliath thrives in churches that are more interested in numbers than the common good. Goliath is at his best behind closed doors, where "insiders" make decisions that preserve power and nourish status.

This Goliath is in each of us, and it is the enemy of those who would follow Jesus. Mark's gospel stands opposed to this Goliath – and screams the objections of Jesus. And those who walk with Jesus don't get it. Jesus and his disciples make their way towards their Jerusalems and, as Jesus speaks, it is the message of Goliath that is heard, a message that has been nurtured in the disciples since their childhood. Jesus tells them what awaits him in Jerusalem – but just like Peter – they refuse to hear his message of suffering and death. They can envision only winning, chasing the Romans out of their homeland, and then being awarded places of honor alongside a celebrated Jesus. And so they argue about which of them will be the greatest. Once again, Jesus takes them aside in order to teach. Instead of repeating the "Get behind me Satan," line he'd thrown at Peter the last time this subject came up, he sits down with his disciples and begins simply. He repeats what he has said for weeks now – that message which confounds The Goliath in us all:

Whoever wants to be first must be last of all and servant of all.

His teaching reverses everything we hold dear. All that the world has taught us is turned upside down. Then he offers a demonstration. He brings a child into their midst – a child – who in Jesus time – had less value than a piece of property – and says, "Whoever welcomes one such child in my name welcomes me." There is silence. "Whoever serves the least of God's people – welcomes me – and whoever welcomes me, welcomes God." And with the saying of those words, The Goliath shudders – but only briefly. For Jesus continues on his journey to Jerusalem, where he is caught in Goliath's web and killed, and for the moment it seems that Goliath has won. But the final word belongs to God. And three days later, the disciples are given a reason to carry on Jesus' fight.

This Goliath is alive and well and the fight continues. Last week National Public Radio aired a story about children in Nepal who are being sold into prostitution across the border in India. The girls are typically between the ages of ten and thirteen, and there are thousands of them being brought across the border each week. The younger they are, the more money they fetch. Thousands of lives are being ruined, as the men who traffic in this "commodity" get rich.

Whoever wants to be first must be last of all and servant of all.

I guess Goliath's words are louder than Jesus'.

Last Thursday, a man arrived here to Saint Paul's, with a soft cast on his leg, who spoke only a few words of English. Turns out he is a migrant worker, who lives in Houston. He was transported here to Norfolk with others who took a job here for a few days. While on the job, he fell off a ladder and injured his leg. He has no insurance; he apparently didn't get paid for the time he worked and had no way of getting home to Houston. His employer decided the best thing to do was to dump him off at the hospital and be done with him.

Whoever wants to be first must be last of all and servant of all.

It seems the employer never heard Jesus' message either.

Last fall I was away at a Christian retreat. It was a wonderful weekend, filled with the words of Jesus – filled with the promise of Christian community. One man on the retreat was a former police officer here in Norfolk, and during one of the breaks we got to talking. He seemed particularly interested in testing my "orthodoxy" on the subject of homosexuality, and as we spoke, I could tell I wasn't passing his test. He then went on to tell me that in the not so distant past, when he was on active duty, a group of officers would drive up to "The Gay Bar" in town, open the front door and let the dogs run in. At the same time, he and several others would be stationed at the back door. As the patrons escaped the onslaught of dogs, they would meet my Christian friend, who would beat them with his nightstick. "Those were the good old days," he said.

Whoever wants to be first must be last of all and servant of all.

The need to be secure is pretty powerful. It seems Goliath is a very real enemy. I guess following Jesus takes more than saying the words, "Jesus Christ is my Lord and Savior."

Whoever wants to be first must be last of all and servant of all.

Understanding Jesus' message doesn't take a lot of education or intelligence. Accepting it, however, requires character. Mark's gospel confronts us today and asks us about our own. The community of those who follow Jesus Christ is to be a community that is different than the world. It is to model different values than the world, values that stand opposed to The Goliath. By living out those different values, we somehow reflect God's presence – Christ's Body here and now. And in the process others are attracted to the unlikely life of servitude and obedience, of generosity and open-eyed sacrifice for the sake of others.

Whoever wants to be first must be last of all and servant of all.

To accept Jesus as Lord and Savior, means to accept him as a very real Savior from the "Goliath values" that eat us alive, a very real Savior from our own self-serving behavior – behavior, which leads to a frightening nothingness – a very real Savior who allows us to live. A Savior who encourages us – *no* – commands us – to live defiantly, confronting The Goliath that is alive and well in the world – and in us. *Amen.*

Out of Poverty

Season of Pentecost – Patricia R. Davis

"Truly I tell you, this poor widow has put in more than all those who are contributing to the treasury. For all of them have contributed out of their abundance; but she out of her poverty has put in everything she had, all she had to live on." Mark 12:43-44

Funny how some small events can stay with you for years after they've happened. It was fully 17 years ago and I still remember it as though it were yesterday. Our girls were little then and I had taken Margaret shopping with me while Genevieve was in preschool. We lived in Pensacola and Rod was often deployed, so I was very frugal with the household expenses, wanting to show him how well I could run our home while he was away. On this morning I had exactly $2.50 left in my purse when I took a break from shopping to sit in the park and feed Margaret. It was then that a rather disheveled woman approached and asked if I knew where she could get something to eat. I really didn't. I didn't know anything about the area churches or soup kitchens, and, being a woman alone, I was nervous of this stranger. But I felt as though my purse had suddenly become transparent, because that $2.50 was an obvious solution. But you know how it goes. I figured it wasn't a good thing to just hand out money; who knows what she might use it for? And surely there were agencies or churches or people more suited to taking care of someone like this. And what little I had couldn't help much anyway. And besides, $2.50 was still $2.50, and I was counting pennies all the time then. So I told her I was sorry I couldn't help and left the park as quickly as I could. On the way back to my car, I passed a coffee shop. In the window was a sign that said, "Breakfast anytime, $2.35."

Rarely are we given so obvious an opportunity to experience the scripture as a living thing, with the power to transform us and the world around us. And so often, we don't see and are content, or maybe just afraid, to let that happen.

Here Jesus is trying once again to open our eyes and so transform the world. Last Sunday we heard the Beatitudes, in which God reveals himself as One who values the least, the lost and the last. Today we have a lesson which echoes that one in which Jesus scorns people of status and authority and holds up a widow as an example of someone dear to God's heart. A widow in that time was a person of precarious status. She had no inheritance rights and, if not taken on by her husband's brother, was dependent on public charity. Widowhood was often such a desperate state that the very fact of it was considered a disgrace. But the ones that Jesus ridicules are those who like "to walk around in [fancy clothes] and to be greeted with respect and ... have the best seats." These contrasting ideas are so offensive ... they seem to suggest that the poor are nearer to God. But there is nothing glamorous or particularly spiritual about being poor. Now, *that's* a sticky point, so we usually take the easy way out and make this into a lesson about stewardship and sacrificial giving. Now, I'm not sure, but I don't think that's what Jesus was saying at all. I think this lesson and those surrounding it are lessons about humility and letting go.

It was the inability to let go that kept that $2.50 in my purse: to let go of my claim on what little I had, to let go of my fear of being found a poor household manager, to let go of my fear of being used and allow myself to be humbled in the face of someone else's need. Humility and letting go ...

Letting go is so difficult and humility such an old-fashioned virtue. Humility carries connotations of a doormat, a meek and rather stupid person who's hasn't the courage to defend herself. It isn't a word that carries much weight in our society and, judging from Jesus' many stories, that's not a new phenomenon. Just the very fact of being alive means that we feel pressured to measure up to a cultural standard, and it's often one of acquisition and achievement, something to offset the gnawing feeling that we are not "good enough." We can become so driven by our need to feel ourselves OK that we can spend a lifetime accumulating and achieving to prove it so. Witness the plethora of self-help books with titles like *Looking Out for Number One* and *Winning Through Intimidation*. Witness the profusion of 20-something dot-com millionaires. Witness the proliferation of huge mansions sitting on tiny plots of land, more and more of them so that everyone can feel special.

So humility may be something that needs another look. It is quite the opposite of accumulation and intimidation. The word *humility* comes from the Latin root word, *humus*, meaning the decayed vegetable matter that feeds plants. It suggests that the very events that humble us, that call into question our worthiness, are the events that may create the fertile soil in which something new can grow.[1] Humility is a word that suggests not an abased and abused attitude but something that is the outgrowth of an examined life. It's the holding of two distinct ideas in tension: first, that we are acutely aware of our sinfulness, our flaws and failings, and second, that we are also acutely aware that we are cherished by God, dearly loved by the Lord of life. Humility arises from being planted in the world but nourished by God's love.

If one of the tasks of this life is to become more whole and more wholly God's, then the very act of giving away what we would hang on to may be one of the paths. But how do we go about doing that and, yes, be good stewards too? There are a couple of ways that I know of. The first was told to me by a friend who went to Calcutta and worked with Mother Teresa for several months. He said that her one rule was that whatever he gave away must be accompanied by the gift of his presence. So, when my friend was approached by a beggar asking for money to buy food, he went with the beggar, bought something to eat and then sat down on the sidewalk and ate with him. It means matching our financial commitment with our physical commitment, so that what we give is the *visible* work of the Church in the world, the hand of Christ reaching out.

The second way to let go of what we have is straightforward, but requires conscious thought every day. It's that each morning before going out the door, we place in our pockets what we are willing to give away that day. And then – give it away! It's an idea that demands deliberate examination of ourselves and equally attentive trust in God. It means

---

[1] Paraphrase from Parker J. Palmer, *Let Your Life Speak*.

approaching each day alert for those who have need of what we have, and then being willing to let it go, for the sake of what God may do with it.

There are all sorts of ways to answer the question of how we care for those in need. Most of the time, the question for us isn't one of being unwilling to give, but of being unwilling to let go. For all kinds of reasons, we cling to what we have: for security, reassurance, pride, control or achievement. There are as many reasons as there are people. Often, what we give away says more about our own need than that of the person before us. We can keep our wallets tightly closed and so close ourselves off from the work that God would do in *us*, or, for as little as $2.50, we can let our lives become transparent to God's hope for all of us. In the end, it may be that giving out of our abundance and giving out of our poverty are really the same thing.   *Amen.*

God Is Not Nice

Season of Pentecost – John J. Capellaro

Stand firm, therefore, and do not submit again to a yoke of slavery... only do not use your freedom as an opportunity for self-indulgence, but through love become slaves to one another.
Galatians 5:1, 13

It seems odd that in this week that we celebrate our nation's freedom, won and sustained with so many hard-fought victories, we are asked to reflect on the subject of surrender. Surrender is a subject we don't handle well. We've been taught from our childhood that our nation's success and the fact of the free world is rooted in victory – not surrender. Surrender just doesn't fit our understandings on how to get through this life. We've even dressed up Christianity with the language of victory. We talk about the victory of the cross, and sing "Onward Christian Soldiers," as if life is about winning. Our religious lore is laced with imagery of royal superiority. How many times have you heard a weary pastor say to a volunteer, "Oh, there's another jewel in your crown for doing that ... ?" as if what awaits in the next life is some Walt Disney produced Monarchy where we and all the people we like being with are members of the royal court, all arrayed in cloth of fine purple and crowns with many jewels, ruling over – well, ruling over all the people we don't like.

We are taught from our first baby steps that the goals of this life will not be realized through surrender. Security, stability, and a tranquil peace are only to be attained through strength, power, and victory. And yet the one we say we follow as Christians has his face set towards Jerusalem. Every step he takes moves him towards Jerusalem – towards

surrender to God, toward confrontation with the powers of this world –
and surrender to those powers – towards death.

And our life of discipleship is a journey *with* Jesus that brings us to the
same fate. If it is security, stability, and a tranquil peace we want, we
certainly don't want to follow Jesus; we certainly don't want to surrender
to God! "Anyone who wants to save their life will lose it ..."

We may long deeply for intimacy with God – but that intimacy begins
with surrender, and that is both foreign to our training in life and
frightening. And so what we long for most, we most resist ... even fear.
I suppose we all know that surrendering to God will turn our lives
around, and move us out of control – and that is frightening.

There is an old Hassidic saying, which I believe captures it accurately:

> *God is not nice;*
> *God is not an uncle;*
> *God is an earthquake.*

Perhaps at some level we all know that, and so it is safer to depend on
ourselves rather than surrendering our trust to God. So we surround
ourselves with things of security, building up our possessions and symbols
of stability. And those possessions need not be only material ones. There
are plenty of spiritual possessions of our own making that offer us
security, all the while keeping us handcuffed to our fears: the trappings
of church or the familiarity of our rituals can become false securities that
assist us in our secret conspiracy to avoid surrender. If we could only
keep things as they are: if we could stay in the same seat, sing only our
favorite hymns; say the prayers that we know by heart – then – maybe
then we could begin to surrender to God.

Yes, Lord Christ, we will follow you, but first let us kiss our families
good-bye; first let us get our affairs in order; first let us have things
arranged the way *we* want. First let us bury our fathers – then we will
follow – then we will surrender to God. Then we will follow your Christ.
First though, please let me get on my Nike's – they're good on long walks;
oh, and I'll need my American Express card in case we pass by a nice
place for lunch, and please we are using the Episcopal Book of Common
Prayer for Compline later, aren't we? Please. Oh please. And Jesus

answers us, "Let the dead bury the dead ... No one who puts a hand to the plow and looks back is fit for the kingdom of God."

> *God is not nice;*
> *God is not an uncle;*
> *God is an earthquake.*

No one knows how hard it is to surrender to God better than Saint Paul. Remember what he admits to the church in Rome? *"I do not understand my own actions. For I do not do what I want, but I do the very thing I hate ..." (Romans 7:15)* But as we surrender to Christ as God's agent, we can experience a new freedom from those fears that control us, from that behavior which serves the self. We can become free from our panicked cravings for stability. Surrender can become a way of life – and although fraught with risk – is also filled with joy, as trust in God becomes something more than words in a prayer. *"For freedom Christ has set us free,"* Paul writes. *"Stand firm, therefore, and do not submit again to a yoke of slavery ... only do not use your freedom as an opportunity for self-indulgence, but through love become slaves to one another." (Galatians 5:1, 13)*

As we surrender and are bathed in God's Light, or in the waters of Baptism, we can begin to be freed from our self-indulgent ways and fears; we can sample a small taste of death to this life, and begin to live in the strength of the community that defines nobility in very different terms than the world does. Within the faith community, a noble life is one that is devoted to serving the other with as much or more energy as serving self. Living a noble life calls us to know our own sins because we have asked "the other," rather than spending our energies finding faults with "the other." The faith community is that collection of broken people who live as if surrender is more honorable than victory.

Christ has his face set towards Jerusalem, then and now ... And so if it's stability we want, or peaceful tranquility or predictability, we may as well build our golden calf now, because that's the only kind of god that we can count on to *not* upset our world. If we can muster the trust and courage to surrender our ways, and walk with Christ together, we should know that we *all* walk towards Jerusalem. And what a walk it is promised to be. This walk guarantees confrontation with the values of this world:

confrontation with our own selfishness and need to be in control, confrontation with our deepest fears, reception into the source of all health and wholeness and coming face to face with the only answer to our deepest longings:

surrender, death and new life.

And if we think it takes less than an earthquake to stir us from our complacency and sense of self-made security, I believe we are mistaken. Thank God that:

God is not nice;
God is not an uncle;
God is an earthquake.   Amen.

Show Me the Coin

Season of Pentecost – Patricia R. Davis

... Then he said to them, "Give therefore to the emperor the things that are the emperor's, and to God the things that are God's." Matthew 22:21

"It's been a quiet week in Lake Wobegon." Garrison Keillor says that at the start of every story about life in his world and I guess a quiet week is a good thing but I've never heard of any nursing homes in Lake Wobegon. It's been far from a quiet week in the nursing home where I work. And since part of my call as your deacon is to bring to the church the needs, hopes and concerns of the world, today I bring you a story from the nursing home about Caesar and God.

But first, let's look at the story as Matthew tells it. It's so familiar that most of us hear it and immediately think of another stewardship sermon. This is a stewardship sermon but it may not be the one you were expecting. In the Gospel lesson, Jesus is approached by some Pharisees who suspected that he was some kind of revolutionary, a serious matter since the country was ruled with a stern hand by Rome. They could expect severe consequences if any rebellion were to spring up and they were determined to avoid just such a conflict between Rome and the Jewish nation. And it's apparent from their remarks that they knew Jesus was not a person impressed by secular power because they said, *... for you do not regard the position of men.* So Jesus was a big question mark and they set out to make him commit himself. In fact, he did, but I think we may have misunderstood his answer. On being shown the coin of the realm, Jesus said, *Render therefore to Caesar the things that are Caesar's, and to God the things that are God's.* We've taken that to endorse the

211

separation of church and state.

According to some, Jesus was here assigning a whole area of life to Caesar or, in our case, the government. The political order, they say, is autonomous within this sphere, while God and the church have to do only with "spiritual" matters. And we can be very comfortable with that; as a matter of fact, the separation of church and state is one of the foundations of our country and one of the things that makes our culture so diverse and open. And life is a lot easier if some things are clearly spiritual things and some are clearly worldly matters and never the twain shall meet. Day to day decisions are so much simpler that way.

But Jesus' answer was, beneath the surface, subversive, because the image of Caesar on the coin was the image of a deity according to Roman culture. So Jesus was asking them to choose who they would have for their god in everything. Not just God on the Sabbath, but God throughout the week, too. Was it to be the god of popular culture, the god who says "go along to get along"? Or was it to be the God of Abraham, Isaac, and Jacob, the God of all creation, who calls us to be co-creators with him? For the Pharisees, it was as Thoreau said, commenting on this passage, that Christ left them "no wiser than before as to which was which; for they did not wish to know." And we too may find it hard to want to know too, but we are in great danger of being Sunday-only Christians if we hold to the belief that this story is about drawing neat little lines around our lives and never letting one part conflict with another.

In fact, we are on a collision course all the time if we have not only "ears to hear" but "eyes to see." And it's not comfortable and it may cost us dearly. From our baptism until our death, we are not released from our vows to "seek and serve Christ in all persons," loving our neighbor as ourselves. This means that we must want, work, and struggle for the same quality of life for others that we want for ourselves. We must do all we can to honor the God-given "dignity of every human being," because in doing so we serve the Christ who is present in each of us. So the separation of church and state comes apart at the seams. Our carefully drawn lines around our lives become dotted lines with great gaping holes where certainty should be. The call to serve God or Caesar gets up close and personal very quickly when we realize that they can both be gods and that we too are called to choose whether we will pay the taxes with our lives or the lives of others. It's not comfortable or easy and it may cost us dearly.

During the week I work as chaplain at a nursing home. It is home to about 220 men and women ranging in age from 35 to 103 who need therapy and a great deal of hands-on care around the clock. The majority are in considerable financial need and most are supported by our taxes to fund their Medicare and Medicaid payments. So the facility has the same concerns as any other business, concerns with profit and loss, concerns with providing care without breaking the bank. And the building itself is aging and a bit run-down, so it needs a lot of work. It lacks a lot of the amenities that most of us would consider necessities, but it still has much to recommend it. The nursing home has a constant schedule of all sorts of different activities and an activities staff that is genuinely concerned that residents are fed intellectually and spiritually. There are nurses, aides and housekeepers who have been there 15, 20 or more years because they love their residents and receive great joy from caring for them. They have more volunteers than I have ever seen any place to help with programs, from the garden club to the Baptist church to Bingo callers. They have given me a great deal of freedom, trust and help in establishing my own ministry in this place. And yet …

And yet, last week I walked the hall, looking to introduce myself to residents I didn't yet know, and I met a man we'll call Joseph. Joseph is an older black gentleman, a really gentle soul who has had both legs amputated because of diabetes. He was in his room sitting in his wheelchair when I met him, and he was very polite and proper, as many people are when they first meet clergy! We got to talking about his stay there and as he talked about losing his legs and coming to stay in a shared room with a strange person in this strange place, he began to weep. He just sobbed from the loneliness of it all and held onto my hand for dear life. It was bare grief and it hurt. So when I got ready to leave his room, I asked if I might come back later and take him to the afternoon activity, so that he could meet some other men. He readily agreed and so a couple of hours later I returned to take him out, but he confided that he couldn't go until he had his bathroom needs taken care of. So I went to the nursing station and told the head nurse, "Joseph needs to be changed so that he can go to activities." Very shortly his aide came up to me and said that she couldn't change him because they didn't have any clean adult diapers; they were still waiting for supplies to be delivered. So I waited around and waited around, half an hour, 40 minutes went by, and Joseph was missing the activity, so I returned to the nurses' station to ask what the problem was. "I'm sorry," she said, "we don't have any diapers so there's nothing I can do." By this time I was on the verge of tears myself, from the sheer infuriating frustration of it all, but I went back to Joseph's room and said, "Joseph, I'm really sorry but I can't seem to make this happen. There aren't any clean things for you right now. Won't you come to the activity anyway? There are lots of people there in the same situation." "I'm sorry, ma'am," he said, "but it's not right for a man to go out in public when he's stinking."

The budget bottom line, job security, the next promotion, the fear of ruffling some feathers ... they are all Caesar when a grown man cries, and it reeks to high heaven.

EXTRA
ORDINARY
TIMES

A National Day of Prayer

Friday, September 14, 2001, Noonday Prayers –
John J. Capellaro

I do not believe that we have permission to sit back and watch and silently wait for events to unfold. As people of faith, we are required to participate in this tragedy and the dialogue it prompts. If religion means anything – if God is real and present in history – then our faith traditions must be relevant in these times of conflict, tragedy, and crises. Like you, I have been moved beyond my wildest imagination to see how tens of thousands of Americans have responded and *are* participating: firemen, policemen, nurses, doctors – volunteers of all kinds digging through debris in hope, determined to participate positively, and in the process revealing a brilliant light. I have been touched deeply to see people driving to airports all over the country opening their homes to strangers who have been stranded, or to see thousands waiting in long lines to donate blood. I, like you, have wept as I have witnessed the sacrifices of so many in our Armed Forces; husbands and wives suddenly separated without so much as a reasonable chance to say good-bye to each other; men and women obediently putting themselves in harm's way for us and for a vision of a safer and better America. And I, like you, have been profoundly challenged to experience America as a nation of prayer – deeply committed to the reality of God in the world and in our lives. As we celebrate this mature and exhilarating moral response from our diverse citizenry, may we Christians take stock of the foundations of our faith tradition.

1. May we reaffirm our allegiance to *God* as the one to whom our primary loyalties belong.

Allegiance to God for all people of faith demands love, compassion, forgiveness, and reconciliation before revenge – however good that revenge might feel.

2.   May we remember that God's ways are higher than our ways, and his thoughts higher than our thoughts.

We cannot know the mind of God. As one professor of mine put it: "If you leave seminary remembering only one thing remember this: God is God and you aren't!" We can only have a glimpse into how we are to live by examining the history of humankind's interactions with the Divine through sacred scriptures, history, and our own experience of God in our lives – and most significantly for us Christians, in the life, death, and resurrection of Jesus Christ. To claim knowledge of God's mind and motives is arrogant, dangerous, and pathetic and is the common ground of all religious extremists, which as we know – leads *only* to the kind of hateful and irrational acts we have seen this week in our great nation. Our own personal need to understand or explain these tragic events simply and cleanly is nothing more than intellectual and spiritual laziness, which leads to further tragedy such as the stoning of our own local Islamic Temple on Tuesday night, or the outrageous claims of one significant local religious leader that he knows the mind and motives of God, and all we need do is follow his personal recipe for a moral life![1]

And finally as the Former Archbishop of Canterbury, William Temple, said just before England entered the Second World War,

3. May we remember that "... *war is both criminal and stupid. Its total effect must be evil, and the suffering it brings is appalling.*"[2]

This is *our time* in human history. If God's Spirit – that is, the Spirit of Jesus Christ – is real – can be embraced as genuine – then we have a

---

[1] This is a reference to Pat Robertson, who claimed that the terrorist attacks were God's punishment for our immoral lifestyles.

[2] William Temple, *Thoughts in Wartime* (London: Macmillan & Company, 1940), 6.

duty – to offer our prayers for an alternative to war. We also have a duty to petition our leaders to pursue the same noble goal. Knowing that if war breaks out, we will be increasingly tempted to hate our enemies. And Christ has said to "Love our enemies."

Meanwhile we pray that God's name be hallowed, and His Kingdom come, and His Will be done in earth as it is in heaven. When we pray that prayer, we do not pray against anyone, but in union with all human beings..."[3] who are precious and sacred children of God. Never before in my lifetime have I been so torn with the very real dilemma of following God's laws of forgiveness and love and the animal level urge to seek revenge. But never before in my lifetime have I experienced the privilege of being an American, among a diverse people who find extremists of all varieties abhorrent, and who remain dedicated to a future of freedom and serving God who is the source of all wisdom and the ground of all hope. This is a time of decision and crises. May we spend this time together in prayer – building our trust in the one Supreme God, whom we have come to know most fully in our Lord Jesus Christ. *Amen.*

---

[3] Temple, *Thoughts in Wartime*, 9-10.

A Terrible Mystery

Diocesan Council – Patricia R. Davis

Then he looked up at his disciples and said: "Blessed are you who are poor, for yours is the kingdom of God."   Luke 6: 20

Sometimes a story tells us the truth when it's hard to hear. And sometimes a story carries the power to change lives. So this morning I tell you a story, a story about a woman who is still changing lives, though she's been dead several years now. This is a true story, the story of a terrible mystery.

And truth, at its heart, always contains mystery. Like the Beatitudes. I don't know if I understand the Beatitudes. Oh, I could tell you what the commentaries have to say. I could explain in detail about the Servant Christ, meeting the needs of a hurting world. These verses have been used for hundreds of years to cheer up the suffering of the world. A sort of pie-in-the-sky kind of justice that is little comfort when your stomach is killing you. Or I could remind you that we may think we have it all together. But really, the Beatitudes are about us too. About how we're all, at one time or another, poor, or hungry, or weeping – if not physically, surely spiritually. All of us spend time at the bottom of life's emotional ladder, but it's not a place we would choose to stay. So, while the Beatitudes make some sort of God-redeeming-the-world kind of sense, I don't much like to dwell on them. Maybe Matthew and Luke, who wrote them down, understood them – maybe the Beatitudes are what got their attention and sucked them in – this notion that God looks kindly on people who haven't got it all together. I don't know. I only know this story.

We met at Norfolk General Hospital. I was a neophyte chaplain, practicing on the unaware and unsuspecting, and she was a patient, and had been for almost 2 months already when I met her. She was to be the one constant in my time there, the one person who remained throughout my four-month internship. She was in her 70's, a large woman with numerous things gone wrong with her body, the result of a lifetime of too much food and too much stress. I visited her every week and, slowly, she began to tell me her story. And as she told it, I heard the Beatitudes, though I didn't like what I heard.

"We were poor," she said, "but I never felt it. Probably because I had such a wonderful mother. She brought me up in the church; she taught me to love Jesus and his mother, Mary. I'm named after her, you see, the blessed Mother Mary, because my mother loved her so much. And whenever we had troubles, my mother taught me to offer it up to the Lord." This was to be the constant refrain, the thread running through her story, just "offer it up to the Lord."

But I, budding chaplain that I was, found her faith hopelessly simplistic and patriarchal. This was a weak-kneed faith I thought, a faith that doesn't wrestle with life and God. How can she live like that, think like that? I didn't understand. But it nagged in the back of my head, *Blessed are the poor in spirit, for theirs is the kingdom of heaven.*

"I got married," she said, "married for years and years. But he wasn't able to be a good husband. He just couldn't stay away from other women. And he wouldn't go to church with me, even after we had the children. He said he didn't need it; that was women's stuff. So I went by myself but he resented it. He used to say I was getting holier-than-thou, with all the going to Mass and stuff. He didn't understand how much I love Jesus, how he's helped me through some really bad times." *Blessed are you when people revile you and persecute you and utter all kinds of evil against you on my account…for your reward is great in heaven.*

"Well," she said, "eventually we separated but we never got divorced. Divorce is a sin in my church. And besides, he was the father of my children. He lived nearby. I saw him sometimes and he seemed to be getting along okay. But it really hurt me that our marriage fell apart because I believe God wants us to love each other, but my husband just couldn't love me. But we stayed in touch with each other, and when he was sick and dying, he came to live with me again so I could take care of him." And I thought this was a woman badly in need of assertiveness training, that she needed to set some boundaries, for Pete's sake. Quit letting people take advantage of her. Couldn't she see that she deserved better than that? Why couldn't she stick up for herself and quit being such a martyr? *Blessed are the peacemakers, for they will be called children of God.*

Week after week we visited like this. She told me her story and I poked and prodded. I pushed her to question, to get angry with God, to show some backbone, to stand up for herself. But she would not be moved. Her faith remained simple and straightforward, her relationship to God unquestioning, her assurance calm. I finally gave up. I continued going to her room but now it was just to sit at the feet of someone with a peace I did not have, and try to understand. She was patient with me. She took me on, as a novice nun perhaps, and attempted to share with me the lessons of her life's journey. I came to find in her room a respite and a sanctuary. I came to use her, like so many others did, as someone who could lift me up and help me out. She encouraged me. In her quiet way, she helped me to be quiet and listen for the voice of God.

And this is what I finally learned. I learned that soon after my internship was over, she was transferred to a rehab facility. She worked hard and grew stronger there and eventually returned to her home in her old neighborhood. There she was known as "The Angel of Hickory Street." It was a title she had earned with her kindness. There was never a neighbor long in need because she was there, offering what she had. Casseroles, prayers, and a helping hand...she gave them all. The neighborhood children knew that they could always get cookies and milk at her house and someone who would listen when everything was going wrong. The bigger kids knew that when they were in need of some extra cash, she would pay a bit for the odd job around the house. One of these bigger kids came to her house one day in search of some spending money and, sure enough, she had some chores that needed doing. He raked the yard, I think it was, and took the few dollars she offered and went home. But later that evening he came back, thinking to rob her and something happened. Perhaps she tried to talk him out of doing this sinful thing.

Perhaps she finally became assertive and stuck up for herself. I doubt it, but perhaps. But something went terribly wrong and this young man, 15 years old, he killed her. An old woman whose life had been hard and who had little to show for it at the end ... he killed her, and his life and mine were changed forever. Because, as he was stabbing her, she prayed for him. At the trial, he said ... she just kept praying for him. He couldn't get it out of his mind. He would never get over it ... an old woman possessed of a terrible, mysterious truth ... *Blessed are the pure in heart, for they will see God.   Amen.*

What on Earth Is Church For?

Preached at Princeton Theological Seminary for The
Princeton Theological Institute, June 21, 2001 –
John J. Capellaro

*I am the vine, you are the branches. Those who abide in me and
I in them bear much fruit, because apart from me you can do
nothing … This is my commandment, that you love one another
as I have loved you.* John 15:5, 12

He has become captivated by the fact of Jesus' life, and the
community which has begun to emerge around his friends. As he grows
in trust, so does his sense of joy about living with a new purpose. There
is a new feeling of freedom he's never known before – and a new energy
to take on the work of this movement he now calls his own. He sees
people made well through prayer; he experiences the power of
forgiveness and sees people change; he encounters new beginnings he
never thought possible. It's as if he's left his former life behind, and is
now living in a mode that yields extraordinary fruit – and *not* of his own
making. This community, this movement, which has embraced Stephen,
seems somehow *engaged* with the Holy. And, perhaps the most
surprising thing for Stephen is that the requisite sacrifices of his new life
are *not* a burden – but rather a privilege. He is filled with exuberance
and a passion for this new life that is contagious. Stephen believes the
wrong things, and so he is killed.

*Those who abide in me and I in them bear much fruit, … abide in my
love … love one another as I have loved you.*

He has become captivated by Church. As Athanasius comes to understand the political landscape of his day, it becomes increasingly clear how he might act on his ambitions. Even though his particular theological understandings are *not* the majority view, he takes it upon himself to make sure that others see things the way he does. This diminutive, redheaded, thirty-year-old Deacon successfully persuades three Bishops of the church to consecrate *him* Bishop in secret. With his new authority, he sends gangs of thugs into the communities of those who disagree with him, burns their churches, imprisons their priests, and even murders some priests whose views are different than his own. Athanasius and his "ecclesiastical mafia"[1] make sure that right belief wins the day. And there are many in the church who believe the wrong things, and so they are silenced or killed.

Those who abide in me and I in them bear much fruit, … abide in my love … love one another as I have loved you.

They have become captivated by the possibilities for evangelism in our neighborhood. Having been given permission to worship in our public high school until they can build a worship space, they begin by canvassing the streets and plastering their messages of fear onto blank walls and telephone poles for blocks around the school. In a neighborhood already filled with churches and synagogues, one ambitious writer from the local newspaper decides to interview the young pastor who is in charge of this new church plant. When she asks him, "Why this particular neighborhood?" the pastor replies, "Because of all the Jews and homosexuals who live in this part of town, of course. We hope they will accept Jesus Christ and be saved from the fires of hell." Many of us still believe the wrong things, and so families will be accosted on their way to synagogue to accept Jesus Christ as their Lord and Savior; posters will be hung in our public schools inviting our children to avoid eternal damnation, and join the *"true"* Christians; and our movement of Christ-like love is once again ruptured into an unrecognizable pool of bile.

---

[1] See Richard E. Rubenstein, *When Jesus Became God* (New York: Harcourt Brace, 1999), 106-107.

226 Searching the Heart of God

Those who abide in me and I in them bear much fruit, ... abide in my love ... love one another as I have loved you.

They have become captives of their own isolation. I received a telephone call recently from the admissions office of a local Christian School, who was considering one of our parishioners for admission. I was asked if I could comment on the family's faith. When I asked "Why?," the admissions director answered, "Well pastor, the parents seemed concerned that we don't teach evolution at this school, and well ... we're just not sure this family is saved."

Do we really think we might not get into heaven if we believe the wrong things? Insistence on "Right Belief" about God, salvation, or any other divine mystery is the beginning of a downward spiral. The first stage in this downward spiral is: *proselytizing and conversion*, i.e., "you cannot live among us unless you become like us"; the second stage is *isolation and expulsion*, i.e., "'you cannot live among us"; and the final stage is *annihilation and extermination*, i.e., "you cannot live."[2] There is too much history of this behavior for us to pretend it's not so.

Is not Salvation being "saved" or "set free" from our selfishness, our addictions, our fears, so that we may begin to live nobly, here and now, living in trust that God's saving hand carries us beyond this life? Does not the Kingdom of Heaven refer to that existence where we acknowledge God as Sovereign and live accordingly – serving the other, loving recklessly, and in our best moments, loving as Christ loved – an existence which begins here and now? Focusing our religion on whatever follows this life seems a great way to avoid the challenges of living as Christ has asked us to now. It's not that the next life isn't important. It just that it's out of our hands. So much of the Christianity I see is less about living in ways that reflect the real presence of God's Spirit among us, and more about saving souls from the eternal BBQ Pit. And our Baptism seems to be less about beginning a new life, forgiven, and strengthened to live nobly, and more about receiving our membership

---

[2] From an article written and never sent to local newspapers by my friend and teacher, the late Rev. Dr. Dennis Kinlaw, in response to our community's dialogue on proselytizing Jews by evangelical Christian fundamentalists.

card, tin badge, and official secret decoder ring in the ranks of the "Salvation Police." Oooooh – Oooohh, I'm in! And you're not!

And then to insist that membership in this club requires a particular set of right beliefs, which of course vary from one chapter of the club to the next ...

Lord do not hold this sin against us... (See Acts 7:60)

Searching for clarity of our belief systems, crucially important though it is, is always a flawed enterprise, and therefore never to take precedence over loving behavior, for Christ's sake! If we need to compel others to be like us, then how can we hope to live lives that bear any fruit? If the role of church is to pronounce "right belief," as if that's the key to salvation, OR as if belief has anything to do with faith, then how does church maintain a commitment to welcoming the stranger, or loving our enemies?

The community from which John's gospel is born offers us a remarkable possibility: that we too, just like those who walked with our Lord in his time, can experience the challenges and joy of his company; that in his company we can live in ways that will be a compelling example to those of good conscience, and thereby the world is changed; and that in our own flawed and frail efforts to abide in Christ, we will see fruits, by God's Grace, and we *will* be living that privileged life of God's Kingdom – here and now. May we encourage one another to this purpose in the Name of the Father and the Son and the Holy Spirit. *Amen.*

About the Authors

John J. Capellaro was raised a Catholic in Philadelphia, escaped church in his teenage years, majored in Religious Studies at Pennsylvania State University, worked in the apparel industry in New York City most of his adult life and came into the Episcopal church in his mid-thirties in order to expose their sons to church, enhance his business contacts, and in hopes of being the first Italian American to be sponsored for membership in the Larchmont Yacht Club! (It never happened.)

He earned his Master of Divinity at the School of Theology at The University of the South in Sewanee, Tennessee and was ordained to the priesthood in 1995. He now serves as Rector of Saint Paul's Episcopal Church in Norfolk, Virginia. He and his wife Bernadette reside in downtown Norfolk with their dogs, Archie and Roscoe. They have two adult sons, Daniel, who is a professional actor and recording artist in Los Angeles, and Lucian, who majors in photography at The Savannah College of Art & Design. Italian cuisine continues to be a significant force in John's life!

Patricia Rhoads Davis grew up on Isle of Hope in Savannah, Georgia amid great oak trees dripping with grey moss. She danced in the Savannah Civic Ballet, majored in Psychology at Roanoke College in Salem, Virginia, worked in a psychiatric hospital and married a Navy pilot. Having been raised in the Lutheran Church, the transition after marriage to the liturgical tradition of the Episcopal Church felt like more of the same mysterious beauty. Patti completed EFM and training at the Virginia Institute for Spiritual Direction before attending the Deacon Formation Program on the campus of Duke University in Durham, NC. She was ordained Deacon in 1999 and presently serves as Archdeacon for the Episcopal Diocese of Southern Virginia, Deacon at St. Paul's Episcopal Church in Norfolk, and Chaplain at a Virginia Beach nursing home.

Patti and her husband Rod live in Virginia Beach with their exceptional cat, Isaac. They have two grown daughters, Genevieve Zetlan, a graphic designer who lives with her husband Scott in northern Virginia, and Margaret, who works as a bank Financial Services Representative in Charlottesville.